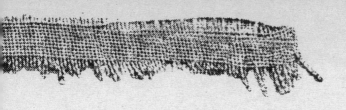

CAT
RUNNING

Zilpha Keatley Snyder

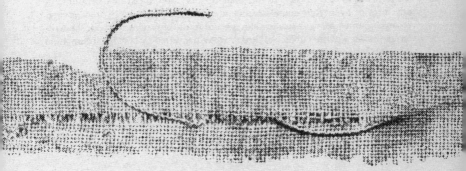

A Yearling Book

Published by
Bantam Doubleday Dell Books for Young Readers
a division of
Bantam Doubleday Dell Publishing Group, Inc.
1540 Broadway
New York, New York 10036

Copyright © 1994 by Zilpha Keatley Snyder

The trademarks Yearling® and Dell® are registered in the U.S. Patent and
Trademark Office and in other countries.

ISBN: 0-440-41152-1

Reprinted by arrangement with Delacorte Press

Printed in the United States of America

April 1996

10 9 8 7 6 5 4 3

OPM

For Larry

ONE

The kitchen was hot and smelled of cabbage and bacon grease and Mama was taking forever to finish washing the meat platter. The smell, along with the knot in her stomach, made Cat feel slightly sick. She swallowed hard and wiped her forehead with the damp coolness of the dish towel, before she leaned closer and whispered, "Mama. He's almost done. Ask him now. Hurry!"

Lunch had been over for half an hour. Or "dinner," as Father still insisted on calling it, even though nowadays, in the nineteen thirties, most people called it "lunch." Cliff and Ellen had walked back to the store ages ago, Mama and Cat had almost finished the dishes, and Father was on the last page of his newspaper. Within a very few minutes he would be leaving too. Going back to Kinsey's Hardware where he would stay, as always on Saturdays, until past Cat's bedtime. "Mama. You promised." Cat nudged her mother's arm.

"Be careful, Cathy," her mother said. "You almost made me drop this platter." Holding the heavy china plate with both hands, she arranged it very slowly and carefully in the rinsing rack while Cat watched, quivering with impa-

1

tience. "It's almost an heirloom, you know. Belonged to your great-grandmother Kinsey."

Cat Kinsey (Cathy or even Catherine to some, but Cat to her friends and in her secret soul) dismissed great-grandmothers and family heirlooms with an angry shrug, and nudged her mother again. Tensing her whisper into an almost silent scream, she said, "Mama! Hurry. He's leaving."

With maddening slowness Mama dried her hands on her apron, and started toward Father. But then, noticing the milk pitcher was still on the table, she picked it up instead. It wasn't until the pitcher was carefully covered with oilpaper, and put away in the icebox, that she again turned toward the center of the room.

Twisting her hands in her apron, she took an uncertain step toward where Cat's father, Charles Kinsey, was carefully folding the newspaper and then arranging his knife and fork neatly across the top of his plate. Cat's heart sank. Mama wouldn't ask him. And even if she did, she wouldn't really argue on Cat's side—even though she'd more or less promised she would.

Father pushed back his chair, straightened his tie, slicked down his bristly gray hair, took his hat from the peg by the door, and settled it firmly on his head. It wasn't until the last possible moment, just as he was reaching for the doorknob, that Mama finally spoke. "Charles. Could I —could Catherine talk to you a moment? She wants to ask you something."

No, no. Cat wanted to shout, *No! You want to talk to him. You promised you'd do it.* But she didn't, of course. Didn't even dare risk a glance that would come close to saying

2

the words that pushed against her clenched teeth. *Mama, you liar. You awful scaredy-cat liar!*

Instead she forced a smile and turned toward her father. "It's about Play Day. Everybody's talking about it at school already and practicing and everything, and I'm going to be in the sixth-grade girls' race and if I win that one I might even win the Winners' Grand Finale, too, like last year." She paused—and avoided the issue for a moment by saying, "Everybody says I'll probably win. I'm a lot faster than anybody at Brownwood, even Hank Belton, and—and everybody says I *have* to win or Brownwood won't stand a chance for the prize money this year." She paused again. Her father's dark eyes were narrowing, his spidery gray eyebrows almost meeting above his nose.

"Yesss?" he said, stretching the word out in a way that made it threaten like a cat's hiss. "Go on, daughter. I know about the fall sports meet. We were discussing it just last week at the school-board meeting. What is it that you want to ask about it?"

Despair tightened her throat. He was going to say no. She knew he was. But she hurried on, the words erupting, tumbling, trying to get out before it was too late. "And everyone, all the girls, everyone but me, they're all going to wear slacks. And I know that Reverend Hopkins preaches against them but Janet says that Reverend Booker says he doesn't think God cares one way or another." *That was a mistake. How could she have been so dumb as to mention Reverend Booker when she knew how Father felt about him? Quick. Change the subject. Tell about—tell about what the teacher said.* "And Miss Albright says that slacks are ever so much more modest when you're doing sports and—''

Her father spoke then, and of course he said no. Well, not the actual word *no*—and not to Cat. Nothing to Cat herself. When he finally interrupted her frantic babbling, he only said to Mama, ''Lydia, why do we have to go over this again? I thought we'd covered the subject quite thoroughly last year. I've told you, and Catherine, too, I might add, that I quite agree with Reverend Hopkins when he says that women in men's clothing are an abomination.''

It wasn't until then that he turned to Cat. ''And over and above the issue of women in men's clothing, Catherine, I thought you solemnly agreed that if you got that green dress you wanted so much you'd not ask for anything more until Christmas.''

''But, Father, this is—this is different. This is because of the race and—and winning for Brownwood—and not being the only girl there, or at least the only girl who's racing who's not wearing slacks, and . . .''

Father turned away. Without even waiting to hear the rest of what she had to say he settled his hat more firmly on his head and went out the back door.

Cat whirled to glare at her mother. ''It's because of the money, isn't it? He just said that about Reverend Hopkins because he doesn't want to admit it, but it's mostly because of the money. He just won't spend a penny he doesn't have to. At least he won't if it's for . . .'' Cat threw down her dish towel and ran.

''Cathy!'' her mother's faint pleading call drifted after her. ''Cathy. Come back.'' Cat kept going.

4

TWO

F ast Cat. Fastest runner at Brownwood School. And almost as good on the high bar and at dodgeball. And when necessary very good at dodging through cluttered rooms as well. Full speed through the dining room, around chairs, bird cages, and plant stands, and on around tea tables and over footstools in the dim, dusty living room. And on to the front door, to burst out into the sunshine— and down the veranda steps in three daring leaps.

Down the steps and across the semicircle of straggly lawn to where the huge fronds of the old palm tree drooped clear to the ground, making a tentlike shelter. A hiding place where, if you stood very still, you were quite invisible to anyone watching from the house. Or even from the veranda steps where Lydia Kinsey was soon standing, still wiping her hands on her apron and calling in her wispy voice. Calling and smiling now, a pitiful pretend smile. "Where are you, Cathy? All I can see is your toes and your hair."

Quoting poetry again, the way she always did. When she was younger Cat had liked to listen to all the poems Mama knew by heart. But lately it only made her angrier when Mama tried to use some silly little kids' poem to make up with Cat after they had an argument. Silly poems like that one that started, *"I'm hiding, I'm hiding, and no one knows where. For all they can see is my toes and my hair."* Trying to make a joke of something that wasn't the least bit funny. She couldn't really see Cat's toes and hair, of course, and what Cat was doing wasn't a joke, or a game either. Or the least bit funny.

Shutting out the calling voice, Cat sat down in the dusty debris near the trunk of the tree. Shutting out, too, the fact that her skirt was getting dirty—or trying to ignore it, at least. After a moment she reluctantly lifted the skirt, brushed it off, and tucked it up into her lap out of harm's way—and while she was at it, the end of her braid. Pulling the long, thick braid of almost red hair—brown, really, but with just a hint of red—forward over her shoulder, she shook shreds of palm fronds out of its curly end. Then, as she often did when she was thinking, she wrapped and unwrapped the curl around her fingers—and concentrated on shutting out the sound of Mama's voice.

Actually, Lydia Shoemaker Kinsey's voice was easy to ignore. Nobody, not Ellen or Cliff or Cat herself, and certainly not Father—particularly not Father—ever paid much attention to what Mama had to say. It was likely, in fact, that no one had ever paid much attention to her, even before she became Mrs. Charles Kinsey. In fact, according to Ellen, that was the reason why she had lost her job at Brownwood School and decided to get married instead.

Cat had heard many stories about how Mama had happened to marry Father, most of them from Ellen. "Skinny little bit of a thing," Ellen had begun just the other night, "right out of teachers college—and with that freckly baby face and carroty red hair, she looked about twelve years old. Should have known better than to take on an upper-grade class like the one here at Brownwood. Fifth through eighth grade it was then, before the seventh and eighth grades went to Orangedale."

"I know," Cat interrupted. "You've told me about it before. Lots of times." She knew all about the year Mama had tried to teach at Brownwood. And how both Cliff and Ellen had been in her class, Cliff in the fifth grade and Ellen in eighth. And how the girls gossiped and giggled all day, and the boys spattered ink and threw spit wads. And nobody bothered to do their lessons or learn anything at all.

"And I'll bet you threw more spit wads than anybody," Cat had said to Cliff. It was easy to imagine what kind of a ten-year-old Cliff had been. Cat was certain, in fact, that neither Cliff nor Ellen had been any help to Lydia. Not that Ellen would ever have been rowdy or giggly, but she wouldn't have been friendly either. At least not after she found out that her own father, Charles Kinsey, head of the "well-known" Kinsey family, owner of Kinsey's Hardware Emporium as well as president of the school board, had asked Lydia Shoemaker to marry him. Had asked the scrawny, nervous little schoolteacher to marry him even though he was almost twenty years older, and had lost his first wife less than a year before.

"She told him no at first," Ellen had gone on to say. Cat had been surprised because Ellen usually tried to make it sound like Mama had schemed and connived to get Father to marry her.

"Hmm," Cat had said in a tone of voice she'd tried to keep from sounding too triumphant. "I guess it *wasn't* all her idea, then, after all."

"Well, not right off maybe," Ellen said.

After Cat considered for a moment she asked, "How do *you* know she said no at first?"

"Father told me so." Ellen had been sewing at the time and for a moment her face disappeared as she lifted the shirt she was mending to bite off a thread. When it appeared again her lips looked thin, and hard enough to snip off thread all by themselves. "She told him she said no because she was worried about how Cliff and I would feel about her taking our mother's place. You know Cliff was only nine when Mama died."

"I know," Cat said. Ellen had told her many long, sad stories about how their mother, the beautiful and elegant Eleanor, had died of pneumonia when Ellen and Cliff were so young.

"That's what she told him," Ellen went on, "but I think it was just that she really didn't want to be a housewife at all. At least, not until she found out what a failure she was as a schoolteacher. So then"—Ellen's lips curled in a spitefully sweet smile—"when she lost the teaching position she decided to try her hand at being a housewife, after all."

Ellen didn't go on to say it, but the way she rolled her eyes around at the living room's dusty clutter made it clear that she meant that Mama had been a failure at that too. But Cat didn't give Ellen the satisfaction of starting an argument about why Mama didn't do much housework, even though there were some things she could have said if she'd wanted to.

She could, for instance, have mentioned that Mama would probably do a lot better if Father wasn't so tight with money. He wouldn't even buy her a new vacuum cleaner when the old Hoover broke down, though he could have gotten one for cost at Kinsey's Hardware. And it was impossible to keep things clean in such a big old house with nothing but brooms and dust mops. In a big old house that, according to Ellen, had once been "the pride of Brownwood"—but was now a leaky, run-down wreck, because of Father's stinginess.

Or she could have mentioned Mama's asthma and headaches, and how little certain people helped out around the house. But if anyone suggested that Ellen might help out more at home they only got a lecture about the long hours she worked at the store, and how Father couldn't get along without her. Arguing with Ellen just wasn't worth the effort.

Cat shrugged, sighed, and leaned forward to peer out between the palm fronds. Mama had stopped calling now and was just standing there wiping her hands and then her pale, freckled face with her apron. She wiped her cheeks and around her eyes, brushed back some flyaway wisps of curly red hair, and then turned slowly and went back into the house.

She probably would go to her room now, hers and Father's, put a wet washcloth on her forehead, lie down on the bed, and have a sick headache. Mama had headaches a lot and most of the time it was when someone had made her feel bad. Like Cat, for instance. Quite often it was Cat. When she was younger it had always made Cat feel terribly evil and guilty, knowing the headache was her fault.

But not anymore. At least not today. Today she was too angry to feel guilty, or to even care whether Mama was

9

going to be sick. Putting all of it, Mama's headache, Father's stinginess, and even the whole problem about slacks and the Play Day races, out of her mind, Cat pushed the palm fronds apart and got into a crouching position. Ready, set . . .

THREE

Crouched and ready to run, Cat waited impatiently for Father to leave for the store. He must have stopped to putter around at the garage workbench again, because she still hadn't heard— But then, there it was, the rasping grind of the starter followed by the clatter and chug of an ancient, ailing motor. Parting the palm fronds, she watched as the old Model A Ford bounced down the rutted driveway, turned out onto the road, and headed for downtown Brownwood. Cat followed its progress through squinted eyes, her lower lip clenched between her teeth. She hated that ugly old Ford. Right at that moment she, Cat Kinsey, hated—everything. And everybody. Particularly everybody.

"I hate them," she said out loud. "All of them." She'd never said it before. Never even thought it, really, at least not in so many words. But somehow saying it out loud made a difference. A jolting difference, like sticking your finger in an electric light socket. She caught her breath sharply, swallowed hard, and ran.

Across the lawn, through a gap in the pyracantha hedge that separated the house from the driveway, and then on down the drive at top speed with her braid flip-flopping against her spine. Around the old garage that had once been a stable, and from there across the field where Cliff's pony had once lived. No pony there now, of course. Not since Cat had gotten old enough to want one. Nothing in the weed-grown horse pasture except Cat herself, galloping fast and free, pushing herself until her lungs burned and her breath came in hungry gasps. Fast and free to the end of the Kinsey property, over the sagging fence, and on across open land toward Coyote Creek.

Somewhere along the way she began to feel, not good exactly, but at least a little less miserable. It always worked that way. There was something about the fiery burn of leg muscles and the good clean ache in her lungs that tended to deaden other kinds of pain. By the time she reached Coyote Creek Canyon her anger had tamed. Something she could direct and control, instead of a dark, raging storm.

The path down to the creek bed was narrow, winding, and very steep. A trail for wild things only. Wild things like deer and coyotes—and Cat Kinsey, whose descent today was a sliding, skittering plunge, checked only by sudden impacts against bushes and boulders until it came to a jarring finish in the creek bed, in an unplanned sitting position. Staggering to her feet she rubbed her bruised bottom and examined herself for other injuries.

Yes. There was a scraped ankle, all right, and that was just one more thing that was all Father's fault. His fault because her leg would have been properly protected if she'd been wearing slacks. And if she got blood poisoning and died that would be his fault too.

Sighing deeply at the thought of the poor youthful corpse lying in state in Spencer's Funeral Home, she

12

limped across a wide expanse of dry creek bed to the narrow stream. At the edge of a pool she squatted and splashed a little water on the smarting scrape, examining it closely for blood-poisoning potential.

Probably not. She skinned her knees and scraped her legs a lot, but she'd never yet had anything more interesting than some pretty spectacular scabs. "Look at yourself," Ellen was always saying. "Your legs look disgraceful. It wouldn't happen if you didn't run so much. Why can't you walk like a young lady?"

Cat shrugged, splashed her wound again, and her face for good measure. Then she got to her feet and started on down the canyon, running again now, flying down the sandy stretches, leaping over rocks and dodging around boulders—until she came at last to the ruins of Monopolis Village. She stopped there and, lying on her stomach on a smooth boulder, stared down at the few remaining traces of roads and walls and thought about the tragic end of the village. And then about other tragic endings, like the end of her friendship with Janet Kelly.

FOUR

Cat and Janet had built Monopolis Village the summer before last when the receding creek had left a small circular pond near the large flat boulder. A deep, clear pond, like a miniature mountain lake. Together they'd planted tiny saplings around the pond on lawns of soft green moss and built twig fences beside sanded roads bordered by shiny white pebbles. The roads had wound through a tiny village where a lot of little green houses and red hotels surrounded a painted tin church. The church had once been a bank for Sunday school money and the houses and hotels were from a Monopoly game. The church, and a lot of the ideas for Monopolis Village, had been Janet's, but Cat had contributed the houses and hotels. The village lasted all summer, until a sudden fall rain flooded the creek and washed everything away.

Cat hadn't been too much concerned about the loss of the houses and hotels. She hated playing Monopoly anyway, and besides, the game really belonged to Cliff, who happened to be the most heartless and greedy Monopoly player in the whole world. But Janet, who'd always had a kind of crush on Cliff, had worried about it a lot. Just the other day, during recess, she'd mentioned it again.

They'd been playing on the bars and Janet was upside down at the time, hanging by her knees. "Hey," she said suddenly. "Do you still play in the creek bed?" And when Cat said she did Janet said, "Do you suppose you'll ever find any of Cliff's Monopoly game?"

Cat did a one-knee spin to a sitting position on the bar. "Not a chance," she said. "They're probably halfway across the ocean by now. But don't worry about it. He still hasn't found out they're gone. Nobody ever played it with him except me, and now when he wants to play I just say I don't want to."

Janet swung back and forth to build momentum and then spun up to sit beside Cat on the bar. "I sure do wish we could play there again," she said. She glanced at Patty Burns, who was hanging from the next bar, leaned close, because Monopolis Village had always been their secret, and whispered, "I really miss playing Monopolis Village. Do you suppose your dad will ever let you come to my house again? Because I know my folks would let me visit you if your dad would let you visit me. Do you suppose he ever will?"

"Not a chance," Cat said again, and Janet made a tragic face, sighed dramatically, and threw herself over backward in a dangerous "dead man's drop."

Cat really missed playing with Janet, too, even though she usually wasn't as dramatic about it. Remembering all the good times they'd had she sighed, scooted forward on the boulder, and dangled her hand down into the cool water of the tiny lake. "Not a chance," she said again, out loud, although there was no one there to hear. No chance she and Janet would be allowed to play together again— except, of course, at school, which hardly counted—because Charles Kinsey wasn't ever going to forgive Janet's father for siding with Reverend Booker.

Cat and Janet's fathers hadn't always been enemies. In fact, a few years back, they'd both been elders at the Community Church. But that had been before Reverend Booker became the new pastor and started arguing with Father about things like having dances for teenagers in the church's social hall.

So then the Kinseys, all except Cliff, had stopped being Community Church members and had started going to the Holiness Church, where Reverend Hopkins felt the same way Father did about things like ballroom dancing and "females wearing men's attire." And because Mr. Kelly had been on Reverend Booker's side, Cat had been forbidden to visit the Kellys anymore, or even to have Janet come to play.

Cat missed having Janet visit, and she especially missed visiting the Kellys, who lived in one of the few new houses in Brownwood, a beautiful Spanish-style stucco with arched windows and a red tile roof. A stucco house with a tile roof—that had been Cat's idea of absolute elegance ever since she could remember. And she also missed the beach cabin at Santa Cruz where, before the Reverend Booker feud, she'd sometimes been allowed to spend several days with the Kellys.

She missed all the movies too. Cat's family went to movies too, of course, when something "worthwhile" was playing, which only happened once or twice a year. But the Kellys went every weekend to the Brownwood theater or sometimes all the way to the new American Theater in Orangedale, where they saw all the latest films—even scary things like *Frankenstein*, and movies that starred actresses with bad reputations and plucked eyebrows. But trips to the movies and the beach were forbidden now. Just as wearing slacks on Play Day was forbidden to Cat Kinsey.

Cat sat up. Resting her chin on her knees, she began again to imagine going on down the creek bed. Past the waterfall and on and on until she reached the river and then maybe even farther, to where the river flowed into the sea. Going on forever, crossing oceans and strange foreign lands and never having to return to the boring little town of Brownwood, and Ellen's mean smile, and Cliff's everlasting teasing, and all of Father's mean, stingy, old-fashioned rules.

FIVE

She'd imagined running away before. Now and then when she was especially angry at all of them, she would spend hours making up long, complicated stories about going down Coyote Creek to the Naranja River and then on down the river to the Pacific Ocean, where she would stow away on an ocean liner headed for wonderful far-away places. She was definitely in the mood to think up a new running-away chapter—if the sun hadn't been quite so hot. But she'd hardly gotten started imagining when she realized that her dress was sticking to her back and beads of moisture were trickling down her forehead.

Sliding down off the boulder she stood for a moment, looking first up the canyon toward home and then the other way, past the rapids and on toward the Naranja and the Pacific. Suddenly she squared her shoulders, clenched her teeth, and headed down canyon.

But just below Monopolis Village was the waterfall. Not a real waterfall so much as a steep cascade, where the water tumbled down over sleek, polished boulders, splashed into a round, deep pond, and then continued on down the center of the widening canyon.

Standing near the edge, Cat peered over, looking for a

safe way down. In all the hundreds of times she had played up and down the creek bed she had gone on past the cascade only once, nearly two years before. A frightening experiment that she had not repeated since.

She'd begun the descent that last time by climbing down the bank on the right side of the stream where a cleft between rocks formed a narrow, ladderlike passageway. Down the cleft and then on to the bottom of the steep slope by jumping from boulder to boulder. Going down had been fairly easy, but when she tried to return it had been a different story. Jumping from boulder to boulder, she discovered, was much harder when the jumps had to be made against the force of gravity. She had been bruised and scraped and pretty scared by the time she'd finally made it back to the top—and she hadn't tried it since. But now . . .

She smiled suddenly—a mocking, bitter smile. What did it matter now if she couldn't get back up? She might be coming back and she might not, and if she couldn't climb the boulders it would just mean that she really ought to run away.

The climb down went easily and before long Cat was on her way downstream again. In new, unexplored territory now, she stopped often to check out deep, quiet pools, gurgling shallows, and interesting rock formations along the cliff face. It was while she was inspecting a pool where some minnows had been trapped by the receding water that she noticed the rabbit.

The creek bed was wider here and a clump of cottonwoods and heavy underbrush had grown up between the stream and the high, rocky cliff to the north. She had been sitting quietly watching the minnows when suddenly a rabbit hopped out from the underbrush, noticed Cat, and quickly darted back the way it had come. Cat went to explore.

The thicket into which the rabbit had disappeared was, on closer inspection, made up not only of bushes and saplings but also of blackberry vines. Vicious, thorny vines that twisted in and out among the saplings, making an impassable barrier. Impassable except by way of the rabbit's tunnel.

The opening was small, not big enough for a human being, even a small-for-her-age eleven-year-old. But Cat was determined. It was definitely a path made by something alive—and the thought was intriguing. She got down on her hands and knees, but the top of the passageway was still much too low. Finally, flat on her stomach, she managed to slither forward into the thicket.

It was slow and painful going. Every foot of the way she had to stop to clear the path, pushing aside sharp rocks and prickly vines. The blackberry vines were the worst problem. Making a tool from a small forked stick, she pushed each threatening tendril back into the underbrush only to have it come bouncing back like a living thing to snag her clothing or stab her arms and legs with its sharp thorns. But she went on crawling and slithering until the underbrush thinned, ended, and she managed to stand erect.

There was no sign of the rabbit but there right in front of her, scooped into the cliff wall, was a wide, shallow cave. A beautiful, mysterious grotto. Her own private, secret hiding place.

SIX

Cat stood absolutely still for a long time, frozen with amazement and delight. It was such an unbelievably mysterious and secret place, and from that first moment she felt that it was meant just for her. As if her decision to go on past the cascade, and to stop at the minnow pond, and the arrival of the rabbit were all part of some deep and meaningful plan.

The cave was wide but not deep. A kind of long, shallow grotto that no doubt had been carved into the cliff face by some long-ago flood. Beneath an overhanging roof of rough gray stone the back of the indentation had eroded unevenly, leaving a number of rocky ledges. The largest, near the deepest part of the cave, was wide and flat, and just the right height to be a kind of bench or bed. The other ledges were smaller and higher up—like shelves. Like nice safe shelves for the storage of the kind of important objects that one would need to keep in a secret hideaway.

She was already beginning to decide which of her most precious belongings she would keep in the grotto. It would be perfectly safe, she felt sure, to keep all sorts of valuable things here. No one would ever find her special treasures in such a well-hidden place. Or find Cat herself, for that matter. No one would ever find her in such a wonderfully secret hideaway.

Tiptoeing slowly and reverently, she entered the grotto. Above her head the rocky gray wall curved up majestically into an arching overhang. She moved on—into shadowed depths where the wide ledge waited invitingly. Scooting up onto the wide, flat surface, she hugged her knees up against her chest. Beyond the wide opening the breeze breathed softly through the thick green wall of trees and saplings. Leaf-filtered light, falling down between the thicket and the cliff wall, spattered the grotto floor with spangles of sunshine. The overhang protected the cave's interior from view if anyone should look down from the cliff above, and the dense thicket of blackberry vines hid it from anyone on the canyon floor.

To find the grotto a person would have to be curious, rather small, and also *brave*. Brave because it took courage to crawl into a tunnel made by who knows what leading who knows where. And brave, also, to endure the vicious scratches and stabs of the blackberry's thorns.

Cat extended her arms and then her legs, noting the many small bloody scratches and punctures. It had been difficult and painful, and because she had endured bravely, it meant that she had earned the grotto. It was hers now—hers alone—and no one else would ever know about it. Not even the rest of the Kinseys. Especially not the rest of the Kinseys. She hugged her knees harder, and her shoulders twitched with a strange, unfamiliar kind of excitement.

It was the excitement, perhaps, that made her forget about her decision to run away. She wasn't sure she'd really meant it anyway. She'd started to run away before and had changed her mind. Running away could come later. For now there was this marvelous, secret place. After a few more minutes of exploring, thinking, and planning, she slithered back through the tunnel and headed for home.

The climb back up past the rapids was much easier than it had been two years earlier, and once she was back on familiar ground, she began to run. By running most of the way there was time, that same Saturday afternoon, to make a second trip to the grotto and begin the first of a long series of changes and improvements.

The first important improvement was to make entering the grotto a little less painful. When Cat arrived back at the blackberry thicket later that day she was armed with some heavy gloves and a pair of garden shears. Before the afternoon was over she had enlarged the tunnel enough to make crawling rather than stomach-slithering possible.

The next step was to transport—in her gathered-up skirt —enough sand to carpet the floor of the passageway to make a more comfortable crawling surface. It was getting late by then but a final project had become necessary, to make the enlarged tunnel entrance a little less noticeable. But that problem was soon solved by bending a bushy young sapling across the opening.

When Cat finally left the grotto the sun was very low. Heading back up the canyon for the second time that day, Cat again ran most of the way.

Mama was awake when Cat got home—and worried.

"Where on earth have you been?" she said when Cat dashed up the back stairs, through the laundry room, and burst into the kitchen. "I've been so worried."

"Just playing," Cat said. "Just playing down by the creek, like always."

"But you've been gone so long and"—Mama paused, and then went on—"and, my goodness, what happened to you, Cathy? You're all scratched up and, look, you've torn your dress. Here, and here too."

"It was a berry vine," Cat said. "I kind of got tangled up with a berry vine." Which was the truth, after all. A kind of truth anyway. Just not a very complete one.

But Mama was satisfied with the explanation. She actually seemed quite cheerful as she went back to the sink to finish opening a can of Campbell's tomato soup.

"Look," she said. "Your favorite soup. Just the two of us for supper tonight. Won't that be fun?"

"Where's Cliff?" Cat asked. Father and Ellen would be eating at the store as usual. On Saturday night, when all the farmers and other out-of-town people came in to shop, it was too busy for them to get away. Too busy for Cliff to get away, too, according to Ellen, but sometimes he did anyway, and now and then he made it home for Saturday-night supper.

"Off to Orangedale with some friends, I think." Mama struck a match, lit a burner on the old gas stove, and began to stir, humming happily.

Cat was puzzled. What was Mama so happy about? And then suddenly she knew. Mama was relieved. Relieved because Cat had been so angry when she ran away. And usually, when Cat Kinsey got that mad she stayed mad for a while. And she would have today, too, if it hadn't been for finding the secret grotto.

But that didn't mean she wasn't angry anymore about the slacks and Father. Because she was. Right now she was too excited about—about other things, but she hadn't forgiven Father, or Mama either. She'd think again later about not being allowed to wear slacks on Play Day. And then she would decide what she had to do about it. Because whatever it was, it was going to be *terrible*.

But in the meantime there was the grotto. Almost every day, at least every day that she could manage a free hour or two, Cat went to the grotto to work on making it even more her own private, secret place. Many times on weekends and in the late afternoon on school days, while Mama was reading or mending or napping and the rest of the family was still at the store, Cat made the trip down the canyon. She ran most of the way, except when she was carrying an especially heavy load. And she always ran all the way home.

Among the first objects that found a new home on the shelflike ledges along the rear wall of the grotto were some of Cat's favorite possessions, like the tiny bronze elephant that had been sent to her by a great-uncle who was a missionary in India. There was also a small white china vase decorated with purple pansies, a very elegant old perfume bottle, a wooden cigar box full of special keepsakes, a collection of fourteen glass, plaster, or celluloid horses, and a few favorite books.

Many of the grotto's larger items came from the Kinsey attic. The attic of the big old house was large, dimly lit, and crammed with old furniture and dozens of trunks and cartons. Rummaging in boxes and ragbags Cat found many useful things, including some discarded quilts and rag rugs that could be used to pad stone ledges and carpet the grotto floor. Among the other items that went to furnish and decorate the grotto were a small round end-table, two folding chairs, a hand-painted kerosene lamp—and Marianne.

Marianne was a big, beautiful doll that had been Cat's present from the family just last Christmas. She was a very elegant and expensive doll with eyes that closed and opened, bristly brown eyelashes, and a head full of stiff, starchy Shirley Temple curls. She was probably the most expensive gift Cat had gotten for a long time and if she'd appeared on the scene three years earlier Cat might have been delighted.

But the thing was, Cat hadn't asked for a doll. She'd mentioned several times that what she really wanted was the pink-and-blue plaid skirt and matching sweater in the window of Emily's Dress Shop. But Ellen had overstocked the expensive dolls at Kinsey's Hardware, and the wholesaler refused to take back the one that didn't sell. Cat knew that was what happened because she'd overheard Father complaining about it.

So Cat got an expensive doll she didn't want from Father and Ellen, and a doll crib that he'd made himself from Cliff, and some handmade doll clothes from Mama. Right after Christmas she had played with Marianne a few times, but she was really much too old for dolls. After a month or two she moved Marianne, her crib, and all her other equipment to the attic. So it was as another attic outcast that the elegant, expensive Marianne went off to beautify the grotto.

SEVEN

Once or twice, during the time she was working on the grotto, Cat came very close to telling Janet about it, but somehow she never did. She didn't know why exactly— except that even if Janet knew about the grotto she wouldn't be allowed to go there with Cat because of their fathers' disagreement about churches and preachers.

And besides, Cat didn't feel quite ready to tell anybody about the grotto. Not even Janet. Someday she probably would, but in the meantime she wanted to go on having it as her own very private secret for just a little while longer.

September was rushing by while Cat was busy furnishing and decorating the grotto, and meanwhile at Brownwood School the excitement about the All District Play Day was building. In fact, as October got closer, it began to seem as if no one could talk about anything else. No one, that is, except Cat.

Cat refused to talk about Play Day. In fact, ever since that Saturday in early September when she'd given up all hope of ever being allowed to wear slacks, she'd refused to even think about it. She knew now—she'd firmly decided—what she was going to have to do about Play Day and the races, but she wasn't ready to tell anybody. Not even Janet.

But in the meantime, with something else very exciting to think about, it wasn't all that difficult to shut Play Day right out of her mind—most of the time. Except for now and then at school when even Janet Kelly, who should have known better, kept bringing up the races and trying to get Cat to practice. As October got closer Janet kept pestering Cat about practicing.

"Let's do a training race," Janet would say at the beginning of almost every recess. And she wouldn't give up, even when Cat told her she definitely didn't want to. Crinkling up her pug nose and doing the cutesy smile that she always used to get her way, Janet would go right on arguing and tugging at Cat's sleeve, trying to pull her toward the playground.

So finally Cat was more or less forced to tell her that she, Cat Kinsey, was not going to run in any of the races. But even that didn't make much difference because Janet obviously didn't believe that Cat meant what she said. Janet, who was absolutely crazy about anyone who was famous, like movie stars and athletes and kings and queens, just found it impossible to believe that anyone would give up something she was practically famous for. Famous, not just at Brownwood Elementary, either, but at the other schools in the district as well. All over the district kids knew about Fast Cat Kinsey and the blue ribbons she'd won at Play Day last year. And the year before that, too, when she'd only been in fourth grade.

But what Janet didn't understand was that Cat had made up her mind that she was not ever again going to be the only runner in the Play Day races who was wearing a dress. And Janet also didn't seem to understand that when Cat Kinsey made up her mind about something—that was it!

One Monday morning Janet was particularly persistent. "Come on, Cat, let's go race," she kept saying, tugging on Cat's arm. "Miss Albright says we should be practicing every chance we get now. Let's race to the back fence. Okay?" Pulling Cat's sleeve and doing her movie-star smile again, she said, "Come on, slowpoke. You're probably all out of practice. I'll bet I win."

Cat grinned back. "Yeah, sure," she said. "Sure you'll win." In spite of the fact that she was almost two inches taller, Janet was nowhere near as fast a runner as Cat. Old pigeon-toed Janet knew she couldn't win any of the races. That wasn't why she wanted to practice. She just wanted to make sure Cat did, so that on Play Day she'd be able to say, "That's Cat Kinsey, my best friend."

Just to shut her up Cat finally said, "Well, okay. Down to the fence and back." But as they left the classroom on their way to the starting line at the edge of the blacktop she added, "This doesn't mean I've changed my mind about Play Day, because I haven't."

"Sure. I know," Janet said, nodding so hard her fat Shirley Temple curls bounced up and down. Fat, round curls that had to be done up on rag curlers every night because Janet's hair was naturally straight. Watching the bouncing curls Cat couldn't help feeling a little bit envious. She and Janet, like most of the girls at Brownwood, absolutely adored everything about Shirley Temple, so it was easy to envy people like Janet who were allowed to take tap dancing and singing lessons and wear short, bouncy curls. Especially since Cat, whose hair was naturally curly, wouldn't even have needed rag curlers—if only Father would allow her to cut her hair.

"Well, I mean it about not being in the races," she said. "And I don't want anyone to watch today either. Okay?" Janet quickly agreed.

On the playground a bunch of girls were playing hop-scotch and some others were practicing backspins and dead-man drops on the bars. Down by the driveway Mr. Alessandro, the janitor, was getting the sawdust pit ready for the broad-jump contest. Nearly all the fifth- and sixth-grade boys were in a clump in the middle of the kickball diamond arguing about something. All except for the new boy, an Okie kid who had just started going to Brown-wood School a few days before.

Dressed in worn-out overalls and the raggedy remains of a man-sized shirt, the new boy was sitting on one of the lunch tables all by himself, swinging his bare feet and staring at Janet and Cat as they went by.

As they headed for the starting line Cat was watching Janet closely to see if she was about to try to get anyone to come watch the race. If Janet yelled, "Hey, everybody. Cat's going to run," or anything like that—that was it. Cat was just going to turn around and march right back into the classroom.

Janet didn't yell anything, but as they were getting on their mark, crouching down at the starting line, it did seem like the whole playground suddenly got a little bit quieter. There was definitely a little less giggling and shrieking from one direction, and not quite as much yell-ing and cussing from the other. Cat almost looked back over her shoulder to confirm her suspicion that Janet had somehow gotten people's attention—except that might look like she wanted them to watch. So she put it out of her mind and tried to concentrate on the race instead. "On your mark! Ready! Set! Go!" Janet yelled, and they were off.

Cat was expecting to be out of practice. Before last year's Play Day she'd practiced nearly every recess, but this year she'd not been racing at all. Not even a quick sprint to get her favorite bar at recess, or the best playground lunch table at noon. So she wasn't expecting to win by very much.

But the minute she started to run she forgot everything except the swift, certain thrill of running. The pounding feet, tingling lungs, and, against her back, the familiar swish and thud of her heavy braid. And, up ahead, the quickly diminishing distance to the school yard fence. Touching the fence, she whirled around and sent her feet flying back in the other direction.

She was almost halfway back to the starting line when she passed Janet, still running the other way. But even Janet's gasping, giggly face barely registered—at least not until Cat had reached the blacktop and slid to a quick stop. Then, as the tingling excitement died away, she gradually became aware of a lot of other things.

Of Janet first. Janet on her way back now, all flopping legs and arms and Shirley Temple curls. A laughing Janet who, when she finally reached the finish line, grabbed Cat and collapsed, dragging them both down onto the blacktop.

"Gee whiz, Cat," she gasped. "Gee whiz." She grabbed Cat again and shook her, panting and laughing, until she got enough breath to say, "You fibbed to me, Cat Kinsey. You *have* been practicing, haven't you? You must have been. You're faster than ever. A lot faster."

"No, I haven't," Cat said, but even as she said it she knew it was only partly true. She hadn't been practicing on purpose, perhaps, but she had been running a lot—stretching her lungs to their utmost and training her feet to fall swift and sure—along the rough, rocky trail to the grotto.

Everybody else said she was faster too. It seemed that everyone had been watching, and as the recess bell rang and Janet and Cat made their way back to the classroom, they all crowded around to say that Cat was better now than she'd ever been. The fastest girl at Brownwood. Probably even the best runner at Brownwood ever—boy or girl. Everyone said so, that is, except the new boy.

The new boy, the Okie kid in the raggedy overalls and bare feet, was leaning against the wall just outside the classroom door when Cat went by. When she just happened to glance in his direction he grinned and said, "Purty fast for a gal, but I could whup you. Real easy."

Cat let her eyes drop down past the worn-out shirt and the knobby bare knees sticking out through the holes in the outgrown overalls—and then on down to the dirty bare feet. She stared at the bare feet for a while before she slowly brought her eyes back up, grinned right into the sharp-boned face, and said, "Sure you could." She didn't say, *Sure you could, Okie,* but she thought about it.

EIGHT

It wasn't until two or three weeks after her discovery of the grotto that a thrilling new idea occurred to Cat. She was in the old garden shed at the time looking for a tool to use in leveling the rocky ledges into smoother, flatter shelves. She had found a small pickax and was about to leave when her eyes fell on something she'd seen so many times it had become almost invisible—a stack of dusty, cobweb-draped wooden panels. But now suddenly she put down the pickax, dashed out of the shed, ran to the house and down the hall to the living room. Sitting down on the floor in front of the bookcase, she pulled out a photo album and leafed through until she found what she was looking for. An old photo of a solemn little girl standing in front of an unusually large and fancy backyard playhouse.

The little girl was Ellen almost twenty years ago, and the playhouse had once stood in the Kinseys' backyard. Father had built it for Ellen from a kit of partly assembled panels that had once been sold at Kinsey Hardware. When nailed together the panels formed an especially elegant playhouse with bright yellow shingled walls, a slanting roof, and fancy wooden trim that made it look like a fairy-tale cottage.

Cat had never actually seen the little house except in the photograph, since it had been taken down and stored away when Ellen got too old to play in it. But she'd seen the dusty panels hundreds of times, sitting there in a neat stack against the back wall of the old garden shed.

Cat put away the album and went back to the shed. Staring at the stack of panels, she was seeing in her mind's eye a quaint fairy-tale cottage tucked away at the back of a secret grotto. It wasn't as if she would be stealing it either. In a way it already belonged to her, because Father had once offered to put it back together for her as a birthday present. At the time Cat had politely refused. For one thing she'd never been the playhouse type. Not the ordinary backyard affair, anyway, with little flower boxes in the windows and, on the inside, doll cradles and cardboard kitchen appliances. And besides, she especially *didn't* want an old secondhand playhouse that had been bought as a gift for somebody else. A secret shelter in a hidden grotto, however, was something entirely different.

It wasn't going to be easy. For one thing, even though the various sections were fairly small, they were much too big to go through the rabbit-hole tunnel. But on her next trip to the grotto Cat found a solution. On the downstream end of the thicket the vines could be pulled away from the cliff face to make a narrow passageway through which the panels could be pushed. That left only the problem of getting them down the canyon.

Although the panels weren't large some of them were quite heavy, and the glass windows were a particular problem. She came close to giving up the whole idea after an almost disastrous attempt to carry a wall section down the first steep trail to the canyon floor. But then the possibility of another route occurred to her.

Not far below the grotto Coyote Creek flowed out of its narrow canyon, under a bridge on the old Brownwood Road, and into the flat land beyond. Perhaps it would be possible to go down the old Brownwood road as far as the bridge, and from there back up the canyon. Now that the new highway was built Brownwood Road was seldom used. Which made it perfect since there would be little danger that she'd be seen by someone she knew.

The very next day Cat went exploring. After reaching the grotto by the usual route she went on past and continued down the canyon. Curving between gradually widening banks the creek soon reached less rugged land. After making its way down a shallow gully in the last wooded slope, it flowed out into the valley toward the Naranja River. And there were no steep drops or boulder-strewn rapids between the grotto and the valley.

Standing on that last wooded hillside Cat could see the line of trees and telephone poles that bordered the old Brownwood Road. And just down the hill was the bridge where the road crossed the creek on its way toward town. It would be easy to come down the road with a wheelbarrow and then, just before reaching the bridge, turn up toward the canyon.

There was, however, one obstacle that she'd forgotten all about until the moment she reached the last slope above the bridge—the Okie camp. From there on the hillside Cat had a good view of it—the cluttered, ramshackle village where a bunch of dust-bowl refugees had been living for the last several weeks while they worked on the Otis ranch. A settlement that most people in Brownwood referred to as Okietown.

Cat had seen Okietown before, but only distant glimpses from the window of a car. Now she was looking directly down into its midst—a straggling collection of sagging tents and shacks made of cardboard and tin, huddled together beside the creek just before it flowed under the bridge.

She moved forward cautiously, being careful to keep behind bushes or in the shadow of a tree. As she got nearer she heard high-pitched voices and saw three small children playing at the edge of the creek. A little farther away a woman stirred something in a pot that hung over an open campfire. There was a mysterious faded grayness about all of it, the road, the tents, the shacks, and the woman and children as well. A lack of color, as if a thin layer of dust covered everything, not only in the houses and clothing, but in the pale, pointy faces as well. Bending over the pot, the colorless woman looked like a thin, ghostly puppet. A witch puppet, stirring her cauldron. Cat shivered.

She'd heard that there were such places all over California these days. Places where dust-bowl emigrants set up temporary camps while they worked on a particular crop, and then moved on when the harvest was in. But how could people live in such an awful way, cooking out of doors and sleeping in shacks and tents without electricity or running water?

Even people, she realized with a sudden shock, that she actually knew. Or sort of knew, anyway. Like that new boy in her class at school. The one with the ragged overalls and the smart-alecky mouth.

Cat shivered again and stepped back farther among the trees. Suddenly she was seeing Ellen's face. Ellen's face with her lips tightening as they always did when someone mentioned the Okies. "Those disgusting Okies," Ellen called them, and she and Father, too, had often reminded Cat not to play with their dirty, diseased children, or go near the terrible filthy places where they lived. The way Father and Ellen carried on, you'd think the Okies were all robbers and murderers.

But Cat wasn't afraid. Of course, she would be careful and not go any closer to the camp than absolutely necessary. If she came this way with her wheelbarrow, she would turn off the road before the camp was in sight, which would make things much harder since the only remaining route was across a plowed field. Not nearly as easy as it would have been if the camp hadn't been right there in the way. Not easy but possible, if she planned carefully.

Because the wheelbarrow trip would take more than her usual hour or two of freedom, Cat planned it for Mama's next Saturday in town. On one Saturday a month Mama rode into town with Father and Ellen and Cliff. On those days she usually helped out at the store for a while, went shopping, and in the afternoon attended the Ladies' Missionary Meeting at the church. When she was younger Cat had to spend such days at the store, too, but recently she'd been allowed to stay home if she had something special to get done. She would think of something special—for school, perhaps. A book that had to be read, or a report to be finished.

The next Saturday morning, as soon as the Model A had coughed and clattered down the driveway, Cat dashed out the back door at a dead run. First to the garage where the wheelbarrow was kept and then, with it bouncing ahead of her, out to the old garden shed. She had decided that she would need only three walls, since the house could be set up so that the back of the grotto would form a fourth. So, by loading carefully, she was able to get all the larger sections tied down across the wheelbarrow. The small pieces she could manage later. After a last testing of the stability of her load, she set off down the driveway.

It wasn't easy. It was a hot day, the wooden panels were heavy, and the huge old wheelbarrow sometimes seemed to have a stubborn mind of its own. Trudging along the shoulder beside the old road, Cat could feel her shoulders aching before she was even halfway to the turning-off place. She stopped to rest once in the shade of the big trees that grew in front of the Ferrises' burned-out farmhouse and again at the edge of the old plum orchard. By the time she finally approached the valley and could see the bridge in the distance, the sun was high in the sky, her face was wet with sweat, and her arms felt as if they were being pulled out of their sockets.

And then, because of the Okie camp, she had to turn off the road and make her way across a field of plowed land —and that was the hardest part of all. Dragging and pushing the heavy load, with the big wheel thumping down into each furrow and having to be wrestled out, she puffed and panted and ached—and clenched her jaws every time she thought about how much easier it would have been if she didn't have to avoid that stupid Okietown.

Next came the short journey up the creek bed to where she could unload the panels and push and pull them through the narrow opening into the grotto. The worst was over then. The trip home with the empty wheelbarrow was much easier. And, in the days that followed, she was able to get all the smaller pieces down to the grotto by the old route.

The next step was to reassemble the pieces, a job which she might never have accomplished if it hadn't been for the instruction booklet that she had found in a heavy envelope tacked to one of the sections. It was just like Father to have attached the instructions to the playhouse in case someone wanted to put it back together. Sometimes Father's careful, methodical ways drove Cat crazy, but this time she had to admit they had come in handy.

Finally, there it was—a small yellow house complete with a slanting roof and three gingerbread-trimmed walls, with a fourth wall of natural grotto stone. A wall that also provided, at the back of the small room, a natural stone bench or bed.

Cat loved the way the house looked sheltering far back under the overhang. Of course, there were sizable cracks between the wooden walls and the cliff face. The door tended to drag a bit, and the roof might be a little bit crooked, but that was only to be expected since she'd not had much experience as a carpenter. It didn't matter anyway. She liked the slightly crooked walls and the sagging roofline. It only added to the mysterious effect.

NINE

The first two weeks of October had come and gone, and Play Day was only a week away, when Cliff brought up the subject at the table—the kitchen table, since the Kinseys had stopped eating supper in the dining room except on Sundays. Cliff and Father were still in their good store clothes, except that Cliff had taken off his coat and tie and hung them on the back of his chair.

Even before Cliff said anything about Play Day, Cat had been eating fast, hoping to leave the table as soon as possible. Mama had burned the carrots and the meat loaf was too raw, and Father had been cross about it. Even crosser than usual. So Mama was being more pitiful than usual. Cliff was obviously in one of his ornery teasing moods. Only Ellen, in her usual neat blouse and skirt and with her dark braids wrapped firmly around her head, seemed the same as always. Not that there was anything particularly comforting about that.

It was the first time any of the family had said anything about Play Day for a long time. Not that Ellen would have mentioned it, ever. Sports in general, and anything Cat was good at in particular, was just something that Ellen wasn't likely to bring up. But last year the rest of the family had discussed Play Day quite a bit, and especially Cat's part in it.

She could recall several discussions about the races and lots of talk about whether Cat had a chance to win any of them. And after she'd won there'd been even more talk, and Father had actually hung her two blue ribbons on the store's bulletin board for all his customers to see and admire.

But this year no one was talking about the races, at least not before that Monday night, and even then Cliff probably only brought it up in an attempt to change the subject. After Father had finished commenting on the raw meat loaf, he started in on the inventory and what to order and what not to order for the next quarter of the year. Father and Ellen were always talking about the inventory.

Cliff was obviously bored. Kinsey's Hardware had always bored Cliff a lot more than it did Ellen, even though they'd both been working there for a long time. In Cliff's case, probably a much longer time than he would have if it hadn't been for the depression. Neither Cliff nor Ellen had been able to get jobs anywhere else when they got out of school, even though Cliff, particularly, had certainly tried. But eventually they both gave up and settled for working for Father at the store. Working for, as Cliff sometimes said, miserable wages but great security.

But having a secure job during a terrible depression obviously didn't keep Cliff from being bored by things like inventory. So while Ellen and Father talked and figured, Cliff fidgeted and squirmed like a little kid in church. And then he changed the subject. He did it at first by teasing Cat—one of his favorite occupations.

He was gobbling down his dessert at the time, which

was only applesauce. The Kinseys, unlike the Kellys, who had cake or pie almost every night, never had real desserts on weekdays—only fruit or bread and jam. Cliff poured some thick cream on his applesauce and then reached over and pretended he was going to pour some on Cat's—because he knew she hated thick cream. She snatched her dish away and frowned at him but he only looked up at her, from under his dark, devilish eyebrows, with a teasing grin.

"Just trying to build up your strength for Play Day, kiddo," he said. "You're going to win all that prize money for Brownwood again, aren't you? I hear the Lions Club is putting up a hundred bucks this year for the winning school, for sports equipment. That'll buy a whole lot of new bats and mitts, won't it?"

Cat took another mouthful of applesauce and swallowed slowly before she said, "I won't be winning anything this year."

"Oh, yeah? Why's that?" Cliff poured another big glop of cream on his few remaining chunks of applesauce and stirred it into a sickening yellow-green sludge. "Some new speed-demon in the running this year?"

"No, I'm just not going to *be* in any of the races," Cat said.

"You're not?" Cliff sounded amazed. "You mean Fast Cat Kinsey is not going to run for the glory of the old Brownwood Academy? Not to mention the family honor." His grin was wolfish. "The first famous athlete in the Kinsey clan in generations and you're going to let us all down?"

Cat only shrugged. Cliff looked around—at Father first

42

and then at Mama—and his grin faded. He turned back to Cat. "You sick or something, kid?" he asked.

Cat scraped up her last bite of applesauce. Then she let her glance flicker toward Father before she said, "No, I'm not sick. I just decided not to be in any of the races this year. Okay?"

Cliff looked again at Father. "You know about this?" he asked.

Father was busy doing his careful end-of-the-meal arrangement of napkin and eating utensils, and for a moment he didn't answer. "No," he said finally. "I didn't know. Catherine hasn't seen fit to inform me that she doesn't intend to be in the races this year. Not until this moment. The decision is hers to make, of course, but"—he turned to Cat—"it would have been thoughtful of you to have told your mother and me before this late date. I've been telling people you'd be running. People ask now and then at the store, and I've been saying you would be competing as usual."

There were a lot of things Cat might have answered. She might have said, *Well, I just decided not to be the only runner who isn't allowed to wear appropriate clothing. Appropriate and modest, too, like Miss Albright says.*

But she didn't say it and she also didn't say that it served him right if he was embarrassed. It served him right if he'd been bragging to his customers about how his daughter would probably win again, and now he was going to be mortified when she didn't even run.

Instead she only looked down and said, "I thought you knew. I thought you knew that I'd have been practicing and talking about it and everything like last year if I'd been planning to run." Then she got up quickly and started clearing the table, biting her lips to keep them from curling into an angry, triumphant smile.

But even though nothing was said about *why* she wasn't going to be in the races, they all obviously knew the reason. Even Cliff seemed to catch on, because after a minute he suddenly nodded and said, "Yeah. Well, I guess I get the picture."

Father didn't say anything more, but as Cat went on clearing the table she could feel his eyes on her. She could feel his eyes and she could also feel a kind of jangly tightness in the room. A tightness that made her wish that someone would say something—or even shout. Even shouting was better than some kinds of silence. After a while Father got up and left the room.

While Cat was helping with the dishes as usual—Ellen never did dishes except on her days off—Mama only talked about other things. She told Cat about a radio program she'd heard, about the best new books of the year, and then she talked about the new novel by Edna Ferber that she'd just started reading. Usually Cat liked talking books with Mama but tonight she couldn't keep her mind on what was being said, and after a while Mama seemed to realize she wasn't listening and stopped.

Later that evening, sitting on the floor in front of the open window in her dark room, Cat leaned her arms on the windowsill and stared out into a calm, clear night. Except for a faint reddish glow over the hills to the west, the sky was a clear transparent black. The ghostly howl of a train whistle drifted up the valley on the night air, from where the evening passenger express was racing through the darkness toward faraway exciting places. Cat shivered.

The thought of being on a train racing off to mysterious new places always made her shiver. She tried to keep her mind on the racing train, but after a while other thoughts started to creep in. She raised her face to the softly breathing night and suddenly blinked away threatening tears.

She didn't want to cry, but whenever she thought about rules that couldn't ever be challenged or argued with, a quick fire burned behind her eyes. And when she let herself remember how much she really wanted to run, and how sure she'd been of winning, there was another mix of anger and pain to swallow—and the anger was partly at herself.

For a long time anger burned her eyes, tightened her lungs, and hurried the rhythm of her heart. She kept thinking how sure she would have been to win, if she were only running—because she *was* faster than ever. In the practice race with Janet she'd known she was faster, even before everyone said so. Faster than ever, even though she hadn't been practicing—except, of course, for all that running back and forth to the grotto.

She might have sat there half the night, wide awake and staring, if it weren't for that sudden memory. The grotto. Suddenly she was there, looking up at the sheltering overhang, and then back at the deep curve of the grotto wall, and, farther back in the shadows, her wonderful fairy-tale cottage. As the sight of it became clearer and more real, her breathing calmed, her clenched hands loosened—and suddenly her eyes were heavy. Leaving the window she crawled into bed and fell asleep.

TEN

On Play Day morning the buses and cars began to arrive very early. Buses full of contestants from the other schools in the district, and cars carrying parents and other spectators. It was going to be a hot day and most of the fathers were in their shirtsleeves and the mothers and teachers were wearing bright-colored summery dresses.

By ten o'clock the school yard, the hallways, and all the classrooms of Brownwood School were full of crowds of people, milling about and talking in loud, excited voices. Everything looked and sounded and even smelled different. Whiffs of perfume, hair oil, and tobacco mingled with the familiar schoolroom smells of books and chalk, freshly sharpened pencils, and stale bologna sandwiches.

Out on the playground the contestants were warming up, throwing softballs and dodgeballs, and racing up and down the driveway and around the track. Cat and Janet walked around watching and talking to people they knew.

Janet was signed up to be in a dodgeball game and, of course, the race for sixth-grade girls. Her Shirley Temple curls were smooth and fat and she was wearing new blue slacks and special low-cut track shoes like the ones worn by real racing contestants. Cat's lips twitched in a secret

46

smile. As if fancy new shoes would be enough to make a runner out of Janet Kelly.

Cat was wearing a dress, of course. And not even the stylish green one with the big square collar that she'd had to do so much whining to get. She'd considered the green one that morning and then decided on an old-fashioned polka-dot thing. If she had to look ridiculous she might as well do a good job of it. Not that any Kinseys would be there to notice. Mama wasn't feeling well and Father had decided that he and Cliff wouldn't be attending the Play Day this year because they were too busy at the store.

She'd been dreading Play Day. Dreading the thought of how different it was going to be from last year, when she had waited all day long for the races, thinking about winning and knowing she had a good chance. But now that the day had started it wasn't too bad. Watching the other events and listening to Janet's excited jabbering was almost fun. And when kids from the other schools saw her and came over to talk about the races, she began to get a kind of spiteful satisfaction out of telling them she wasn't going to run. And when they asked, "Why? Why not, Cat?" she only said, "Because I don't feel like it."

The dodgeball games weren't until eleven o'clock and, as always, the races were in the afternoon, so Cat and Janet watched broad jumping for a while, and then the softball throw, cheering for the kids from Brownwood School. But Brownwood wasn't doing too well. All the first-place winners were from Lincoln or Elwood. But then Carl Monroe, Brownwood's best pitcher, won first place in the softball throw and that helped some.

When it was time for the sixth-grade dodgeball game, Cat went over to cheer for Janet—briefly. As usual, Janet was put out on about the third throw. She ran across the ring once or twice, dodged the wrong way as usual, got hit, and came out of the game giggling—also as usual. That was another strange thing about Janet. It never seemed quite natural to Cat that a person could care so little about winning or losing.

Lunchtime was more noisy confusion, with kids running around looking for lost lunch pails and sitting down to eat in usually forbidden places, like in the sawdust under the bars, along the hall railings, and even out on the front lawn. Lots of kids were lined up at the tables in the back hall, where the PTA mothers were serving cookies and lemonade. And a big bunch of people, kids and parents, too, were buzzing around the official scorekeeper's booth trying to find out who had the most points and which school might be going to win the Lions Club's money. The rumor was that Brownwood was in second place just behind Elwood.

The most popular event, the races, finally began about two o'clock, and as always the primary girls came first. A Brownwood third grader, Marybeth Higgins, came in second, not that it mattered all that much. Of course, Marybeth's points would help Brownwood a little, but nobody was too interested in the little kids' races, especially the ones for girls. Then came the primary boys, and after that the upper-grade races began—the fourth graders, the fifth, and finally the ones everyone was waiting for—the sixth graders and then the Winners' Grand Finale.

It was very strange watching the sixth-grade girls take their places at the starting line. Standing on the sidelines Cat kept her eyes on the runners, ignoring the stares and comments. Things such as "Look. That's Cat Kinsey. You know, the girl who beat Joe Shaffer last year."

Ignoring, too, the shouted questions. "Hey, Kinsey. You broke a leg or something?" Or "What's the matter, Cat? Did you get disqualified?"

Then Mr. Sloan, the principal from Lincoln, shouted, "Get on your mark. Ready. Set. Go." And they were off and, in her imagination, Cat was off too—heart pounding, muscles twitching, breath coming faster and faster. But when it was over and a long-legged blonde from Elwood had won it, Cat just had to get away. She forced herself to wait until Janet came puffing and panting back to the finish line. She even managed to congratulate Janet—for not coming in dead last. But then she just had to leave. Telling Janet she had to go to the bathroom she forced herself to walk slowly across the playground. She wanted to run. To run and cry and scream with anger.

In the girls' rest room she washed her face with cold water again and again and then just stood there leaning on the basin—until Janet stuck her head in the door.

"Hurry up, Cat," Janet said. "The boys' race is about to start. Come on. Let's go."

"Look," Cat said, "I'm going back to the classroom now. I've got some stuff I need to do before I go home. Why don't you go on out and watch and—"

Janet stared at her in amazement. "Cat. You can't go now. You can't miss the sixth-grade boys' race and the Winners' Grand Finale. That's the most fun of all."

The winners' race. The Grand Finale, in which the first- and second-place winners of all the other races, both girls and boys, ran against each other. And the race that, to

49

everyone's total amazement, had been won last year by a very small fifth-grade girl—Cat Kinsey.

Cat shrugged. "I don't care. Nobody from Brownwood is going to win anything. None of our boys can beat that big guy from Elwood."

"I know," Janet said. "They probably can't. But we've got to stay and cheer anyway. For Hank and Benny. Maybe they'll win if we cheer loud enough."

Cat gave up and let Janet pull her down the hall and out onto the playground. Pushing through a bunch of parents and teachers and pulling Cat behind her, Janet managed to get a place for the two of them in front, only a few yards from the starting line.

It was a long line. Winning races—as well as winning all that new sports equipment for their school—seemed to be especially important to sixth-grade boys. There were boys of all shapes and sizes in the line. Boys that Cat had known, and beaten in races, all of her life. And boys from the other schools that she knew slightly or only by sight. And then down at the very end of the line she saw someone else—the new Okie boy. Dressed in the same old ragged overalls he wore every day—and as barefooted as ever—the new boy was crouched down, preparing for the start of the race.

Somebody snickered and Cat looked around and saw that other people were noticing the Okie kid too. Noticing and grinning and pointing—pointing particularly at his bare feet. But he didn't seem to see the pointing—or anything else. As he crouched at the starting line, his tight-skinned, bony face tipped upward, his eyes were as blank and empty as if he were blind. Cat was still staring at the blank eyes when the starting gun sounded and they were off.

At first there was only a wild jumble of swinging arms and pounding feet while a mind-numbing roar rose up from the sidelines. People screaming, "Hurrah!" and "Yippee!" "Yeah, Benny!" and "Go it, Jesse!" Or simply hooting and screeching in an ear-splitting explosion of noise.

Cat didn't remember the noise from last year, at least not when she was running—as if the running had shut her away in a silent world of speed and strain. But now she put her hands over her ears and winced. Winced, blinked —and then blinked again and shook her head, refusing for a moment to believe what her eyes were telling her. Refusing to believe that, out in front of the thudding, flailing pack—way out in front and widening the distance with every stride—was the Okie boy. His bowl haircut flopping wildly, his skinny face taut and shiny with sweat, the Okie boy was winning the sixth-grade boys' race—in his bare feet. And half an hour later he won the Winners' Grand Finale—beating the tall Elwood boy by several yards.

Watching the Okie kid flying down the track in his tattered shirt and bare feet, Cat hated him. She had never hated anyone so much in her whole life.

ELEVEN

Brownwood School cheered some for the Okie kid, but not right off. Not during the sixth-grade race, anyway. In that race there was, at first, only a kind of gasp. A shocked, breathy gasp that seemed to come from everywhere, followed by a stunned silence. And even when the cheers began there wasn't a great roar. Just a few scattered "Yahoos" from Brownwood kids when they realized that, to their surprise, their school had just won five points— and maybe even stood a good chance to win the ten points that would go to the school that took first place in the Winners' Grand Finale. And therefore, a good chance at all that Lions Club money.

There was more cheering for the Grand Finale. By then, half an hour later, a great deal of talk had happened. All over the Brownwood playground people had asked, "Who is he?" and "Where did *he* come from?" And "Does he really go to Brownwood School?" There had been answers from the few people who knew, and before long the answers were everywhere. "Yeah, he goes here. He lives in the Otis ranch Okietown down the old Brownwood Road. Calls himself Zane, or something like that. Yeah, that's it, Zane Perkins. Yeah. Hurrah for Zane!"

And by the time the winners from all the races were lining up for the Grand Finale a lot of people, at least a lot of Brownwood people, were shouting, "Atta boy, Zane. Go it!" And "Show 'em your heels, Zane." But right then, louder than all the other voices, some Elwood kid yelled, "Yeah, Okie. Your bare heels!" And a lot of people laughed.

But the new boy didn't seem to hear any of it, not the cheering, or the insults and laughter either. Running like before, as if he were blind and deaf to everything outside himself, he beat out the Elwood champion by several strides and everyone else by yards and yards.

Cat waited only until he crossed the finish line before she pushed her way through the excited crowd and hurried to the sixth-grade room. In the cloakroom she got her sweater off its hook and was reaching up for her lunch pail when she suddenly stopped and stood perfectly still, biting her lower lip and breathing deeply.

All alone in the privacy of the cloakroom—breathing in the familiar atmosphere of library paste, sweaty clothing, and stale sandwiches—she tried desperately to shut out the sound of cheering from the playground. Shut out the cheering and the anger too. To swallow and smother the wild, aching rage she'd felt when the Okie kid won the Grand Finale. But it wouldn't go away. Grabbing her lunch pail off the shelf she ran down the empty hall, out the front door, and down the street.

Later she remembered heading for home, but she found she couldn't even be sure which route she'd taken. She couldn't clearly recall if she went the way she was supposed to, the long way, the half mile on School Street and then along Burks Lane to the old Brownwood Road. Or if she'd taken the forbidden shortcut over Three Sisters' Ridge—which she sometimes did when she was in a hurry. She didn't think she'd run much of the way either —but she wasn't even sure of that. But whichever route she'd gone, she eventually got home and went directly to the kitchen, as always, to wash out her lunch pail and put it away in the pantry. She was getting out a clean dish towel when Mama came into the room.

"Cathy. I didn't know you were home already," she said. She put her hand under Cat's chin. "Your face is all flushed. And you look exhausted."

When Cat turned her face away Mama hurried to the sink to fill a water glass and then to the icebox to chip a thick chunk off the block of ice. But then, as she handed Cat the cold glass, it began, just as Cat knew it would. The questions about Play Day.

Cat pulled out a chair and sat down. She swirled the glass slowly and carefully and then sipped the icy water before she answered, "Fine. Everything went fine."

"Oh, I'm so glad." Mama took the colander off the sinkboard and went to the pantry for potatoes. Cat waited, pressing the cold glass to her cheeks and forehead. Mama had washed the potatoes and started to peel the first one before she asked. "And—and did you race?"

"*No*, I wasn't in any races." Cat paused to take another sip of water. "I meant it when I said I wasn't going to run."

"Oh, I see." Mama was on the second potato before she went on. "And the prize money? Who won the Lions Club prize money?"

Cat shrugged—as if it hardly mattered, at least to her. "Brownwood, I think."

"Didn't they announce the winner and give out the ribbons, like last year?"

"I guess so. I didn't stay to find out for sure. But this kid from Okietown—the one I told you about who's in my room? Well, he won the sixth-grade boys' and then the Winners' Grand Finale. So we probably got the prize money."

Telling about the Okie boy made the anger come burning back, and the sound of it must have been in her voice, because Mama put down the potato she was peeling, turned around quickly, and stared at Cat with a puzzled frown.

"No, I'm not angry about it," she said when Mama asked. "Why should I be angry about it?" Then she slammed down the empty glass and left the room. Halfway down the back steps she came back to say, "I'm going for a walk. Okay?" She didn't wait to hear the answer.

She ran most of the way. So hard and fast that the anger, as so often happened when she ran, was soothed or perhaps smothered from lack of air. But she knew it was still there. She felt it seeping back the moment she reached the grotto. Hurrying to the cottage, she went in and slammed the door behind her. Sitting on the padded stone ledge, hugging her knees against her chest, she could feel it oozing like liquid fire behind her eyes and beneath the skin of her face. But after a while it began to fade and other thoughts and questions began to seep through—questions she didn't want to ask and thoughts she didn't want to deal with.

She wanted it back now, the burning hatred that she'd felt before. Wanted it back to burn away the troublesome questions that were turning the pure, clean anger into something ugly and spiteful. Squeezing her eyes tightly shut, she reminded herself of all the things she'd been thinking on the way home from school. Thoughts that fed the angry flames like kerosene on a burning log.

What right had he to run in the Brownwood race, anyway? To run in the school race and win the prize money for Brownwood, as if he were really a part of the school and town, instead of just a dust-bowl beggar kid who lived in a dirty shack in that terrible shantytown? What right had he and his whole family to even be here in California, living on land that didn't belong to them and probably stealing things every chance they got, just like Ellen always said? And how could he possibly have the nerve to run—out there in front of everybody—IN HIS BARE FEET!

That was the worst part. That, she suddenly knew, was what made her angriest of all. The fact that he'd had the nerve to . . . But she didn't want to think about that. Her mind was just starting to pick at the idea the way you pick at a half-healed scab, to skirt around the edges of why it made her so furious that even though he had no shoes and must have known that everyone would laugh at him, the way people always laughed about anyone who didn't wear the right kind of clothes—only worse, much worse. Bare feet was certainly worse than . . .

It was right then, at that very moment, that she began to be aware of a strange scraping noise. A noise that was coming from just outside the door of the cottage. Something seemed to be pulling on the door, trying to open it. Trying and then trying again, while the door squeaked and scraped and refused to budge.

The slightly crooked door had always been hard to

open, and when you slammed it hard, as Cat certainly had when she came in, it took a good strong yank to get it started. Cat sat still as death, hugging her knees harder and harder, as the unseen hands tugged and pulled and tugged again. But then it began to give, scraping out slowly over the rough, rocky floor.

It scraped once more and suddenly it was open and there, standing in the doorway, was a very little boy. A ragged, filthy little boy no more than four or five years old was standing right there in her own secret, private grotto, staring at her with wide, frightened eyes.

TWELVE

For only a moment the dirty little ragamuffin stared at Cat before he caught his breath in a strangled gasp and disappeared. He was there and then, almost in the blink of an eye, he wasn't. Shocked, stunned, and strangely frightened, Cat sat as if turned to stone for long frozen seconds before she could even begin to think sensibly about what she had just seen.

Her first reaction, the weird feeling of fright, wasn't sensible at all. There obviously wasn't anything dangerous about a tiny little kid, even a ragged, dirty one. A little boy only a few years old wasn't anything to be afraid of, of course. However, there was a lot to fear if he was from Okietown, because now that he'd discovered her grotto he'd probably tell everyone. Tell all the terrible thieving people in that awful place and . . .

Suddenly coming to life, Cat came down from the ledge and across the cottage in one flying leap. She shot out the door, glanced quickly around the grotto, and then crawled frantically out through the tunnel. She ran downstream at first, pausing only when a boulder or bush or clump of saplings offered a possible hiding place. As she darted around boulders and pawed her way through bunches of underbrush, she finally calmed down enough to ask herself what she would do if she found him. What would she say and do if, rounding this next clump of saplings, she came face to face with the dirty little Okie trespasser?

At first she didn't have any idea—but she soon came up with one. She would scare him. She'd grab him—shake him—yell at him—tell him that if he ever came back, if he ever told anybody she'd . . .

That was about as far as her plans went, but as it turned out it didn't matter anyway, because the little boy seemed to have vanished as if by magic. He wasn't anywhere downstream, or upstream as far as the rapids. Nor was he still hidden somewhere around the grotto thicket, which she explored much more carefully when she finally returned to where the search had started.

It wasn't until she arrived back inside the grotto, breathless and angry and frustrated, that it occurred to her to check to see what damage the kid might already have done, and how many of her belongings he'd already stolen. Realizing that when she'd arrived that day she'd been so upset that she might very well have failed to notice such things, she began a careful inspection.

The two highest shelves would be beyond his reach, but by standing on one of the folding chairs he probably could reach those as well. But nothing seemed to be missing. The pansy vase, the perfume bottle, and the books were in their proper places. Even the horses and the elephant, things that would probably be the most tempting to a little boy, stood just where they'd been before.

And inside the cottage, too, nothing seemed to have been disturbed. The blankets on the ledge, the rug, as well as the chairs and table and kerosene lamp, were just as they had been. She was beginning to think that perhaps the little boy had just found the grotto—had only stumbled onto it today, and by chance onto Cat herself—and hadn't had time to steal or destroy anything. She had almost convinced herself that was the answer, when she remembered to look at Marianne.

The doll crib—a cradle, actually, that Cliff had made out of an old golden oak rocking chair—was sitting below the ledge, just where Cat had left it. And Marianne was there, too, under the pink doll blanket. Marianne was there; but not just as she had been before.

As Cat pulled back the blanket she immediately noticed that something was, not missing, but different. The difference was a flower, a wilted Indian paintbrush, lying on Marianne's chest and, tucked in beside her right hand, a small withered apricot. And Cat knew, beyond any doubt, that she herself had never left a flower in Marianne's crib, and certainly not a rotten apricot. So the boy had been there before, and would no doubt be back.

Cat went out to the edge of the grotto and threw the flower and apricot as far as she could into the thicket, and then she went back to sit on the ledge in the cottage. She sat there for quite a while feeling terribly worried—and at the same time, in a strange, unexpected way, almost relieved.

She didn't recognize it as relief right at first. She was almost home before she began to be aware of the faint undercurrent of satisfaction that oozed in and out among her feelings of anger and worry about the grotto trespasser. Satisfaction, she gradually came to realize, because she wouldn't have time now to even think about Play Day.

She would have to forget about all that. About the races and the Okie kid, and why his bare feet had made her so angry. All she would do now, could possibly do, was concentrate her energy on protecting the secret grotto. She would have to spend all her time planning and plotting—as well as standing guard every possible moment—if she was going to save the grotto from the little Okie trespasser.

So, beginning the next day, Saturday, and again on Sunday after church, she spent long hours standing guard over the grotto—and at the same time avoiding any discussion of Play Day with her family. To her surprise nobody mentioned the races, or argued about her being gone so much. It was as if they could see she was feeling bad and they knew—well, Father did anyway—that it was his fault. So for whatever reason, when she said, "I'd like to play down by the creek today, okay?" or "I think I'll take a long walk this afternoon," nobody argued. So she waited in the grotto every possible minute. Waited and watched, but no one came. And there was no sign that anyone had been there either. No more flowers or apricots.

But then Monday came and another school day and for a while the whole Play Day topic was impossible to avoid no matter how much she tried to keep her mind on other things. At school everyone was talking about Zane Perkins and what a fast runner he was.

"Hey, Cat," Hank Belton said the minute he laid eyes on her, "I'll bet Zane could beat you too." Of course Hank would be the one to say that. He'd always hated it that a girl could run faster than he could.

"No, he couldn't," Janet said. "Cat could beat him any day. Couldn't you, Cat?"

"Oh, yeah? Why don't you try it, then? Why don't you and him race?"

And a lot of other people started saying the same thing. "Yeah! Swell! Why don't you race him, Cat?"

And when she walked away they said, "What's the matter, Cat? You afraid to try? Yeah, she's chicken. Cat Kinsey is chicken to race against the Okie." And some of them even started saying, "Cat's afraid to race with Zane." Calling him by his name as if he were another regular Brownwood kid and maybe even a friend. A friend, just because he was a fast runner.

That sort of thing went on all day but Cat just ignored it. Most of the time it wasn't too difficult. She just wouldn't talk about racing or even look at people who were talking about it. She wouldn't look at Zane Perkins, either, except for once when the teacher called him to come up to the board to do an arithmetic problem.

She had to look at him then, wearing another ragged shirt and a different pair of ragged overalls. Too big for him this time instead of too little, with baggy bottoms and a crotch that hung down to his knees. But then he turned around and she found herself looking at his broad face with its strange, uncivilized eyes, dark and deep-set eyes under pointy eyebrows. He grinned then, right at her, and she had to quickly pretend to be staring at the problem he'd done on the board. Studying the problem and smiling sarcastically as if she'd caught him making a dumb mistake.

The next few days she hurried home from school and, as soon as she could, on down to the grotto. She didn't always get there as soon as she'd like to because Mama, who usually didn't pay much attention to what she did after school, was beginning to ask a lot of questions and make all sorts of suggestions.

"Cathy dear," she'd say with a worried look on her face, "don't you want to help me with the darning today? You used to say you thought darning socks was fun. Remember how we used to see who could recite the most poetry while we were darning?" Or other times she'd ask what it was that Cat did every day down by the creek. But after Cat had made up enough long, boring stories about building dams and catching tadpoles, Mama finally gave up and let her go.

Every day that week—Monday through Thursday—she spent at least an hour at the grotto, without seeing any sign of the trespasser. But on Friday there was a teachers' workshop in the afternoon and classes were dismissed at one o'clock. So Cat crawled in through the tunnel about two hours earlier than usual. Earlier than usual and earlier, obviously, than the trespasser expected her to be— because the moment she crawled out of the tunnel, got to her feet, and looked around, she knew that he was there.

THIRTEEN

It was mostly just a feeling that warned Cat that the trespasser was right there in the grotto, a mysterious feeling that something was wrong. Almost as if she had suddenly developed mystical powers, like clairvoyance or second sight. Clairvoyance, most likely.

Of course, the fact that there was a strange object sitting there in plain sight just might have helped too. But she'd definitely started getting the mysterious feeling before she even noticed the pail. A stained and rusted pail made out of an old Shell oilcan with a makeshift baling-wire handle that was sitting just outside the cottage door.

But whether the warning was by way of second sight or oilcan it served its purpose, and Cat was able to make her next move very carefully. Holding her breath, she tiptoed across the grotto and, as she neared the cottage, sank down to her hands and knees. Beneath the side window she rose up gradually until she could see over the sill. And there, inside *her* cottage, her own *private, secret* cottage, was the same little boy.

Sitting on the floor beside Marianne's crib the ragged and dirty little trespasser was rocking slowly back and forth. Cat could see the back of his bowl-shaped haircut and the bottoms of his dirty bare feet sticking out from under his raggedy backside. His hair was sun-streaked brown. There was something strangely familiar about the color—and the homemade haircut as well. A mental image of a boy's back as he stood at the blackboard flashed in Cat's mind and resentment flared up into anger. Jumping to her feet she jerked open the cottage door.

As the door screeched open and banged back against the wall, the little boy jumped up, his eyes wide with fear. Still clutching Cat's doll against his chest he retreated backward until he bumped into the wall.

"Okay, kid," Cat yelled, "what do you think you're doing? This is my house and you're a trespasser, and trespassing's against the law. I'm going to tell the sheriff and have you put in jail."

The boy shook his head violently. He seemed to be saying something but his lips were trembling and his voice was very faint. Big, fat tears began to roll down his cheeks. He started edging sideways, keeping his eyes on Cat as if he expected her to jump on him at any moment, like a terrier after a rat. When he got to the crib he sank down beside it.

Looking up at Cat he moved his lips again, and this time she could make out most of what he was saying. In a high, trembly, babyish voice he said, "I ain't hurt her none. See, I ain't hurt her." He unwrapped the pink blanket and held the doll up for Cat to see. "See? She ain't hurt a bit. I was just playing with her a little. I was just playing. . . ." The trembly voice broke down in a rush of sobs and the kid bent his head and buried his face in Marianne's blanket.

As Cat stared down at the sobbing little kid she began to experience a puzzling sensation. A sinking, shriveling feeling—like an inner tube with a nail in it. All the righteous, burning anger was fizzling out, leaving in its place a strange swollen kind of ache that made it hard to swallow and that made her eyelids tight and hot.

"Hey," she said over the painful lump in her throat, "you don't have to cry about it. I'm not going to tell the sheriff. At least I won't if you promise not to come here again. Do you promise not to come here again? And not to tell anyone about this place, ever? Do you?"

The kid cried awhile longer before he raised his face. Still sobbing and with tears streaming down his cheeks, he stared up at Cat. His lips moved but no words came out. Then he looked back down to where he was still clutching Marianne against his chest, and cried harder than ever. So hard, it occurred to Cat that he might be going to strangle and die right there before her very eyes. Then he looked up again and in a wobbly wail said, "Awright. I promise. I won't tell nobody. And I won't come no more." He looked back down at Marianne and sobbed. "I can't come back no more. Not ever no more." And he buried his face in the pink blanket again.

"Kid," Cat said, and then louder, "hey, little boy!" But the kid went on crying—and on and on. It wasn't until she practically shrieked, *"Hey you!"* that his head jerked up. Staring at his tear-wet face Cat said sternly, "What do think you're—why are you—how'd you . . . ?" And then a little less sternly, "What's your name, anyhow? You got a name, don't you?"

He nodded, sobbed, whispered something that sounded like "Sammy," and went on crying.

"Sammy?"

He sobbed and nodded.

Cat sighed. Okay. So his name was Sammy and he was about five years old and . . .

"Sammy," she said, "tell me something. How the dickens did you find this place, anyway? And how come you're way out here all by yourself? Don't you have any folks to look after you?"

Sammy turned loose of Marianne with one hand and wiped his face, smearing dirt and tears across his cheeks. Then he sobbed again, hiccuped, and nodded. "I got folks. But my ma and pa been pickin' ever day, so I stay with Granny Cooper. Granny Cooper don't go pickin' so she's mindin' me."

Not very well, Cat thought. "Well, then," she said, "if Granny Cooper is minding you, where is she now? Right this minute. How come she's not taking care of you right this minute?"

Sammy stared at Cat for a moment. Then his large wet-lashed eyes looked off thoughtfully into the distance and his lips moved in a way that might be just the hint of a smile. "Sleepin'," he said. "Granny Cooper sleeps a whole lot." The almost smile faded. Then he looked down at Marianne and whispered something Cat only heard a part of—a part that sounded like "good-bye" and then "Lillybelle."

"Lillybelle?" she asked. "Did you say Lillybelle?"

He looked up guiltily out of the tops of his eyes and nodded. "I jist calls her Lillybelle. My ma had a doll named Lillybelle onced. Not a corncob one neither. A real store-made doll like this here one."

"Her name," Cat said firmly, "is Marianne."

He nodded. "Marianne," he said. He looked down again, said "Good-bye, Marianne," and then added in a whisper, "Lillybelle." Then he put the doll into the crib and carefully tucked in the pink blanket.

It was right then, at that moment, that something— something about the look on Sammy's small, pointy-chinned face as he tucked in the blanket—made Cat almost certain of something she had already begun to suspect. "Sammy," she said, "you're a girl, aren't you?"

Sammy looked up, startled—and worried. "I didn't tell," she said. "I didn't tell you, did I?"

Cat grinned. "Samantha, I bet. Samantha?"

Sammy nodded guiltily. "I ain't supposed to tell folks, though. Not till we get back to Texas. Or when I go to school. Ma says I can be a girl agin when I start goin' to school."

"Why does she say that?" Cat asked. "Why doesn't she want you to be a girl now?"

"I don't rightly know," Sammy said. She looked down at herself. At the baggy, ragged shirt and overalls. "Ma says we ain't got no money for girl things right now. So I got to wear what don't fit Roddy no more. And Spence too. Sometimes I get to wear Spence's growed-out-of things too." She ran her hand down the sleeve of the blue plaid shirt she was wearing—a much-too-big blue plaid shirt with both elbows out and a frayed collar. "This here shirt was Spence's," she said proudly.

Cat started to say it was a good-looking shirt but the thickness in her throat suddenly returned, making it hard to talk. She'd found herself remembering the boxes of old dresses she'd run across in the attic when she was looking for things for the grotto. Dresses that she'd outgrown long ago and that were, for the most part, pretty old and faded, but a lot better for a little girl than the ragged scraps of a boy's shirt.

After a moment she swallowed hard and asked, "You got two brothers? Spence, and what did you say the other one's name was?"

"Roddy," Sammy said. "Roddy's the littlest one. And the meanest." Then she suddenly smiled. A full-out shining smile that showed white baby teeth and dented her dirty tear-streaked cheeks. "And Zane too," she said. "I got a big one too—name of Zane."

Cat felt a kind of collision somewhere in the middle of her chest, as if a swallow had tangled with a breath going the other way. "Zane?" she said, and as she said the name she could feel the anger rising up, burning away the swollen softness in her throat. She stared down at the ragged little Okie for a moment before she said, "You better get out of here, right now. You get on home and don't you ever come back."

The little girl edged around her and out the door. Halfway across the grotto she turned and looked back.

"Go on. Get!" Cat yelled. "Scat! And don't you ever come back or I'll call the sheriff."

Sammy turned and ran.

FOURTEEN

When the little Okie reached the tunnel she galloped down it on her hands and feet like a monkey, instead of crawling the way a larger person had to do. No wonder she'd gotten away so quickly that other time when she'd seemed to disappear as if by magic. In no time at all she was out of sight. Cat turned back toward the cottage—and noticed the pail again.

The beat-up old oilcan pail was still sitting just outside the cottage door. Inside the pail were three walnuts, a small shriveled orange, and a chunk of very stale bread. Cat poked at the stuff with the tip of one finger. The kid's lunch, no doubt, or maybe—Cat smiled ruefully—some more gifts for Marianne. For Marianne-Lillybelle. Suddenly Cat ran toward the tunnel.

It was slow going crawling through the narrow passageway carrying a pail, and when Cat got to her feet outside the thicket there was no one in sight. But the kid couldn't have gotten far. "Sammy! Wait a minute!" Cat yelled, and started to run. She'd only gone a few steps when, dodging around a large boulder, she came to a skidding stop and jumped back. But it was too late. They'd seen her.

Leaning against the boulder, her heart thudding, she

heard someone say, "Well, well. If it ain't Cat Kinsey," and a moment later there he was, Zane Perkins. And not just Zane. Behind him was what seemed to be a whole crowd of smaller Zane Perkinses. A regular herd of ragged, barefoot little Okies in scruffy overalls, all of them grinning in the same ornery way. All grinning, that is, except Sammy, who still looked tearful and terrified. Grabbing Zane's hand Sammy tugged at it and whimpered, "Come on. Let's go home. Please, Zane."

Cat stepped away from the boulder casually, as if she'd just happened to jump back there to look at something and hadn't been trying to hide at all. As the mob of Okies crowded in around her (four of them, actually—it had seemed like more at first) she lifted her chin and calmly stared back into the grinning faces. Then she held the pail out toward Sammy. "Here," she said, "this must be yours. You forgot to take it with you. You left it up there—beside the creek. *Right up there by the creek*," she repeated loudly, hoping to remind Sammy that she'd promised not to tell anyone about the grotto.

They all looked at Sammy and Sammy looked at the pail. Reaching out timidly as if she were afraid that Cat might grab her, she took it, looked in it, and started to cry again.

Zane was frowning. "What's the matter?" he said. "What're you bawling about?" Then he turned to Cat. "What's Sammy bawling about? You do something to Sammy?"

Cat sighed indignantly. "Of course not. I didn't do anything to her—" She caught herself and changed it to "to him." But the damage had been done. Zane glared at Sammy and she cried louder.

"Her?" Zane asked. "She calling you *her*, Sammy?"

"I didn't tell her," Sammy wailed.

"She didn't tell me she's a girl," Cat said, "if that's what you're talking about. I just guessed."

But Zane went on frowning. "Sammy," he said, "Ma told you and told you—"

"Look," Cat said, "it's not her fault. And besides, it's pretty stupid to think it's all right to let her run around all by herself all day, just because she's dressed like a boy. What's she doing way out here alone, anyway? No kid that little ought to be way up here all alone, whether she's a girl or a boy."

His grin was mocking. "You some kind of expert on rearin' young-uns?" he asked. Then he grabbed Sammy, wiped her face with her shirttail, and said, "Shh. Hush up now. I ain't going to tell Ma." He wiped her face again and bent over her, whispering something in her ear.

While Zane was still talking to Sammy one of the other boys came up to Cat. It was the one next biggest to Zane— the same coloring and lanky build. And the same dark-framed eyes, too, but maybe not quite so devilish looking. "Sammy warn't left all alone, she jist run off," he said. "This here old lady in the camp s'posed to be mindin' her, but she ain't doin' too good a job, I guess. When Zane and Roddy and me got home from school jist now Granny didn't know where Sammy'd got to. But I knowed she likes to play up thisaway, so we come a'lookin' for her." He grinned at Cat. "Right glad you found her."

Cat examined the grin for sarcasm but didn't find any. "Who're you?" she asked warily.

"Spence," he said. "Name's Spence Perkins."

Cat nodded. She vaguely remembered seeing him before

at school. Third grader, she thought, or maybe fourth. "And the other one. What's his name?" She looked for the smaller boy and suddenly noticed that he'd disappeared. "Where is he, anyway?"

"Roddy." Spence looked around. "Where'd he git to now?" Turning in a circle he called, "Roddy!" several times. When he'd turned back around to Cat his raised eyebrows and shrug said something like *That's Roddy for you.*

Just then Zane, who'd been talking to Sammy, got back into the conversation. "Where'd Roddy go?" he asked.

"Don't ask me," Spence said. "He was here a minute ago. Must of gone thataway. I'll find him."

Watching Spence disappear around the boulder Cat suddenly froze. The tunnel was only a few yards away and she hadn't taken the time to bend the sapling screen back down over the entrance. What if . . .

"Hey," she yelled. "Come back here." But at that moment the littlest boy came dashing back. Grabbing Zane's arm he yelled, "Come 'ere, Zane. Come quick. Wait'll you see what I found."

Cat's heart sank. "Hey," she said. "Don't . . . Come back here. You can't . . ." But no one was paying any attention. Ignoring Cat altogether they followed the prancing, grinning Roddy around the boulder, past the first small clump of saplings, past the beginning of the thicket —and right to the entrance of the tunnel. Dropping down to his hands and knees he disappeared down the narrow passageway, and as Cat continued to protest, the others followed one by one. Zane first and then Spence and then Sammy too. Sammy, too, but not before she'd stopped at the tunnel entrance, looked back at Cat, rolled her big eyes wildly, sobbed, hiccupped, dropped to her hands and feet, and started after her brothers.

Cat followed. There was nothing else she could do.

Inside the grotto they were everywhere, picking up the elephant and the horses, looking at the books, and running in and out of the cottage.

She couldn't stand it. "Stop it!" she screamed. "Get out! Get out of here. Get out of here or I'll tell the sheriff."

They stopped, but only for a minute. Roddy put the elephant back on its shelf—and then picked it up again. Spence came out of the cottage and then went back in. Zane strolled toward Cat, doing his wide, mocking grin.

"This here your property?" he asked. "Your pa got papers on this land?"

Cat had to consciously unclench her teeth in order to answer. "No. Not on this land. But all this stuff is mine. I brought it here and I built the house, and it's mine. And my father knows Sheriff Dunn real well and if you don't get out of here I'm going to tell him you're all a bunch of thieves and he'll put you in jail—and throw your folks out of Okietown"—Cat's voice was getting higher and more shrill—"and expel you from school and . . ."

Zane didn't try to argue. Instead he just stood there nodding slowly and doing his insulting grin. When Cat finally stopped to catch her breath he made a kind of snorting noise and said, "Well, if you're anywheres near runnin' down I got a thing or two to say. First off, we got no interest in coming back here. Roddy and Spence and me ain't got no interest in playin' house or"—he nodded toward the shelves at the back of the grotto—"or fooling around with little-kid stuff like that. Ain't that right, Roddy?"

Roddy looked at the elephant regretfully for just a moment before he reached up to put it back on the shelf. Then he swaggered over to stand beside Zane. "That's right." He pulled himself up to his full seven- or eight-year-old height. "We got no use for kid stuff like that," he said. "Huh, Spence? Huh?"

Spence was walking toward them. He was holding a book in his hands, but when Zane and Roddy turned to look at him he put it behind his back. "That's right. We got no use for—"

But just then Zane interrupted. "Where's Sammy?" he said. He looked around the grotto and then at Spence. "Where's Sammy? She was here a minute ago. Wasn't she?"

Spence shrugged. "In there," he said, nodding toward the cottage, "with the playbaby."

She was there again, all right, just like she'd been before, sitting on the floor beside the crib with Marianne-Lilly-belle in her arms. Just before he got to the cottage door Zane had been saying again how none of the Perkinses had any use for Cat's "little-kid stuff," but he stopped talking when he saw Sammy with the doll.

They stood there for quite a while before Zane stopped watching Sammy and looked at Cat instead. "Hey," he said. "Who knows? Maybe won't none of us come back here no more, and then agin—maybe we will. You gonna sic the law on Sammy, Cat Kinsey?"

FIFTEEN

On the way home from the grotto that day Cat told herself that, of course, those Perkinses would come back again. Any kid, finding such a wonderful place not far from home, would go back again and again. And actually, Okietown wasn't any farther from the grotto than the Kinsey house, and by way of a much flatter and easier trail, besides. They'd probably keep coming back until all of Cat's things were stolen or broken unless . . . She hated to even think of taking all her things away and leaving her wonderful private place empty and deserted and at the mercy of those thieving Okies, but perhaps that was the only thing to do. But then again, maybe it wasn't.

There was one slightly comforting consideration, and that was the fact that the Perkins boys were all in school. Which meant they would only be able to go to the grotto when school was out. And that, of course, was when Cat could be there too. When she could be there to chase them away or at least stand guard over her belongings. And she would too. Every spare minute after school and on weekends she'd be right there seeing that they didn't do any damage.

Of course, that didn't solve the problem of Sammy, who

apparently could go to the grotto anytime the old lady who was supposed to be taking care of her happened to take a nap. Sammy would be the biggest problem.

The answer might be to take Marianne away. If the doll wasn't there, maybe Sammy wouldn't be so apt to come back. That was it. Cat would bring Marianne home from the grotto and put her away again, back in the attic where she belonged.

As she trudged up the canyon Cat thought some more about Sammy. About how she had held the doll, and the look on her face as she tucked in the pink blanket. At first, thinking about the way Sammy looked at Marianne made Cat angry. After all, Marianne belonged to her. She'd been her Christmas present just last year and she was a very expensive doll. It didn't matter that she herself had never been all that crazy about dolls in general, or Marianne in particular. Marianne still belonged to Cat Kinsey and Sammy had no right to even touch her, and that was all there was to it.

But the memories of Sammy's face when she looked at the doll, and also of the way her face looked as she tucked in the blanket, kept coming back. And somehow, by the time she'd scaled the steep canyon wall and was crossing the empty pony pasture, Cat had decided to wait awhile before she took Marianne away. She'd wait to see if there was any sign that Sammy was doing any harm, like losing Marianne's clothes and messing up her beautiful, almost human hair. She'd let Marianne stay in the grotto for the time being, but she'd sure enough keep an eye on things that might get damaged.

She did too. The next day and the next, when Cat came to the grotto the first thing she did was to check on Marianne. She inspected the doll carefully, looking at her hair, her dress, and her shiny black shoes—but nothing seemed to be disturbed. All that week everything seemed to be the same as always—at least in the grotto.

It was everywhere else that things were different. Starting on that Monday it began to seem to Cat that her whole life was suddenly full of Perkinses. Perkinses on the way to school, where she'd twice seen Zane and Spence and Roddy as she walked up Burks Lane. Perkinses on the playground at recess, where she kept noticing Spence and Roddy—Roddy running and yelling with some other second-grade boys, and Spence sitting on the railing outside the third- and fourth-grade room. Just sitting there alone usually, reading a book or watching some other kids play marbles.

And a Perkins in her own classroom, too, of course, where Zane's seat was only one row over and two seats back from her own. And where, every time she turned around, there he was, looking at her. Looking at her and grinning or at least twitching the corner of his mouth as if he were threatening to. The same way he twitched his mouth whenever—and it happened all the time—somebody started teasing Cat about being afraid to race with him. The teasing went on and on. Cat hated it.

"Afraid!" she finally yelled at Hank Belton. It was during the noon recess on Wednesday and he'd come over to where Cat and Janet had been practicing dead man's drops on the bars. It was obvious that he was there just to tease and be ornery. Hank was the worst—the one who just wouldn't let the subject drop.

"I'm not afraid to race anybody," Cat yelled at him. "I just don't feel like it. And it's none of your business anyway, Hank Belton." Cat could feel her face getting hot and she knew her voice was screechy, but she didn't care. Marching right up to where Hank was standing at the edge of the blacktop, she stood on her tiptoes so she could yell right into his face.

"I know what your trouble is, Hank Belton. Everybody knows what's getting your goat. You're just mad 'cause you can't beat me. That's it, isn't it? You just hate being beaten by a girl."

Hank's pale lumpy face went shiny red and he raised his hand as if he might be going to take a sock at Cat. Raised his hand, clenched his fist, and— Just at that minute a ball whizzed by and then something came crashing into Cat and Hank, too, almost knocking them both down. It was Zane Perkins.

"Hey, sorry 'bout that." Zane was talking to Hank, hanging on to his arm and kind of brushing him off as if he might have gotten him dirty or something. "I was jist tryin' to catch that there ball. Warn't looking where I was going, I guess. You ain't hurt, are you?"

Cat regained her balance and, with her hands on her hips, glared at Zane. He didn't even seem to know that he'd run into her too.

Janet came over then and whispered something in Cat's ear. "He threw that ball on purpose and then ran after it. I think he was just trying to run into you, or maybe Hank," Janet said. She thought for a minute and then added, "You know what I think? I think he might have been trying to keep Hank from hitting you."

Cat rubbed her ribs, which had been whacked by some-body's bony elbow in the collision. "So? He'd rather hit me himself, I guess," she said. Zane went right on talking to Hank—talking and apologizing and not even looking at Cat. So Cat ignored him back, and went on ignoring him every chance she got. And not just him but all the rest of the other dumb kids who kept suggesting that she and Zane ought to have a race to prove who was the champion of Brownwood School. As if an Okie who wouldn't be here after the grape harvest ended could be counted as a real Brownwood School student.

It was on Thursday afternoon that Cat began to suspect that Sammy was still coming to the grotto after all. On that day, like all the others, Marianne was just the way Cat had left her—or maybe not. Cat wasn't entirely sure but it seemed like the blanket was folded a little bit differently. So before she left that day she set a trap. She tucked a very small leaf into a fold of the blanket right under Marianne's chin so that the leaf would fall out if anyone moved the blanket. And when she came back the next day the leaf was gone. Marianne's dress wasn't dirty or messy, and her yellow curls were still neat and crisp—but she had definitely been played with. Played with and then sneakily put back in the crib just the way she'd been before. Well, Cat Kinsey could be sneaky too.

SIXTEEN

It took quite a bit of thought to come up with a really good plan, but by Friday morning Cat had it all worked out. Unfortunately, to make it work right she might have to tell a lie, or something pretty close to it. However, if everything happened *just* the way she had it planned, it wouldn't have to be a complete lie, in which case it would be only a little bit sinful.

She went to school as usual that morning, but during the first recess she gave up her turn on the bars, which was practically unheard of for Cat Kinsey. And during lunch hour she didn't even go out to the playground. Instead she just moped around in the classroom, picking up books and putting them down, and staring out the window. "You go ahead," she told Janet, who'd come back in to look for her. "I think I'll just stay in the room and read or something."

"Come on, Cat," Janet said. "Look. I've got gum." Miss Albright didn't allow gum in the classroom, but it was all right on the playground if you remembered to park it somewhere before you came in.

Cat almost weakened. It was spearmint, her favorite. "I'll take some for later," she said, taking two sticks out of the pack. "I don't feel very good right now."

"You don't?" Janet peered at Cat with narrowed eyes and then nodded knowingly. She felt Cat's forehead with the back of her hand and asked her to stick out her tongue. Cat sighed and rolled her eyes. She knew that Janet was planning to be a nurse someday, but she sure could be a pest when she started acting like she thought she already was one.

"Come on, Cat. Stick out your tongue," Janet went on nagging, so Cat stuck it out, all right, but not the way you're supposed to when a doctor is looking at it.

Sure enough, it didn't take Janet five minutes to go tell Miss Albright that Cat was sick. Cat had known she would. Janet was a great one for telling teachers everything that came into her head. It worked out just the way Cat had hoped it would. All she had to do was nod her head when Miss Albright asked her if she was sick, which made it only half a lie, since she didn't actually have to say any of the words herself.

"Perhaps I should call your family doctor," Miss Albright said. "It's Dr. Wilson, isn't it? Do you want me to call Dr. Wilson?"

Dr. Wilson had been the Kinseys' doctor since Cat was born, and he was a friend of the family too. Not quite as close a friend as he had been before he voted to keep Reverend Booker at Community Church, but he was still the family doctor. Cat definitely didn't want to see him at the moment.

"I think my mother had better decide if I need to see Dr. Wilson," she said quickly.

"Would you like to just go on home, then?" Miss Albright asked.

Cat sighed and said she did. Which wasn't a lie at all.

She started off, back to the cloakroom first and then down the hall, at a slow, sickly walk. But as soon as she was out of sight she began to run. Just before she climbed over the fence to Burk's apple orchard she stopped long enough to take a stick of gum out of her sweater pocket and pop it into her mouth before she took off again at top speed. Out across the orchard and on up the hill that led to Three Sisters' Ridge and the shortcut home. And when she got there she didn't even have to go inside, since Mama wouldn't be expecting her for more than two hours. Instead she hid her books and lunch pail under a bush and went on running.

Just like before, Cat knew as soon as she crawled out of the tunnel that someone was there. And just like before it felt like second sight would have told her, even if there hadn't been any other clues. As if the grotto was so much her own personal, private place that there would always be a kind of angry shiver in the air if an intruder had been there.

The angry shiver was there, all right, but this time the other clue was simply the cottage door. It was standing a little bit open and she distinctly remembered closing it firmly the last time she was there. Getting slowly and quietly to her feet, she stood still for a moment getting ready, breathing hard and clenching her teeth and fists. This time she was really going to scare that dumb little Okie so much she'd never, ever come back again. Silently rehearsing all the awful scary things she was going to yell, she tiptoed up to the cottage window.

Just like before Sammy was sitting on the ground near the doll crib, but this time she was holding Marianne out in front of her, making the doll stand on its feet. And talking. Talking and talking. Cat couldn't quite make out the words, but whatever she was telling Marianne-Lillybelle, it was quite a long story. As she talked she tipped her head from side to side, smiled, frowned, and once or twice even laughed out loud. Once in a while she'd stop talking briefly, nodding and cocking her head as if she were listening. Then she would be off again, chattering away like a mockingbird.

Cat didn't want to be fascinated—or even interested. She was, though, because, for one thing, watching the fluttery-eyed smiles and frowns, she couldn't imagine how, even for a minute, she'd taken Sammy to be a boy, just because of dirty overalls and a boy's haircut. And for another thing she found that the small, big-eyed face, and the dimple— most especially the dimple—were definitely putting her in mind of somebody. Somebody who—and then she knew. Shirley Temple! And when Cat slammed open the door Sammy's round-eyed frightened stare was a lot like Shirley Temple too.

"All right," Cat said in a tone of voice that didn't come out quite as threatening as she'd meant it to be. "I thought you promised never to come back here again. You broke your promise. Didn't you?"

Sammy had jumped to her feet, still holding Marianne out in front of her. Her chin was trembling and tears were beginning to ooze out of her eyes.

"Now stop that," Cat said quickly. "You don't have to do that again. I'm not—I'm not going to hurt you, so you can just stop it. Stop that crying this minute."

Sammy seemed to be trying, sniffing and blinking and swallowing hard—and then sobbing again. Trying to get her mind on something besides bawling, Cat said hastily, "What were you talking about? Just now to Marianne? I saw you from the window. What were you saying to her?"

Sammy swallowed, looked down at the doll and then up at Cat. "I was jist tellin' Lillybelle about how it's goin' to be onced we get back to Texas. I was tellin' her 'bout our house—and 'bout the chickens and the pigs."

It was working. As Sammy got into her story her tears and sobs disappeared as if by magic. "And 'bout the baby jackrabbit Zane caught for me. The littlest ol' rabbit, no bigger than nothin'—when I got him, anyways. I was telling her how we'd git us another baby rabbit like Hoppy, onced we get back to Texas and—" She stopped suddenly and stared at Cat with widening eyes. "I didn't mean it when I tole her I was goin' to take her with me. I was jist playin' like. I was jist playin' like she was goin' back to Texas with me."

It looked to Cat as if Sammy was building up to another good crying spell if something didn't happen. Taking her hand Cat pulled her back to the ledge and lifted her up onto it. Then she scooted up beside her. Still clinging to Marianne-Lillybelle, Sammy stared at Cat, big eyed.

"So," Cat said in a friendly-chat tone of voice, "I want to hear about your house in Texas. Why don't you tell me all about it? I don't know much about Texas except that Austin is the capital. Did you live anywhere near the city of Austin?"

Sammy stared at her, blinked hard several times, and stared some more. Cat folded her hands and put a patiently waiting expression on her face. But Sammy went on staring—at Cat's mouth.

"What are you staring at?" Cat asked finally.

Sammy swallowed hard, leaned forward, and peered into Cat's face. "You got some chewin' gum?" she asked.

Cat, who had forgotten about the gum, took it out of her mouth and looked at it. "Yeah," she said. "Spearmint. Spearmint's my favorite."

Sammy was staring at the gum. "Do you swaller it when you're done chewin'?"

"No. Of course not. If you swallow gum it makes a lump in your stomach and stays there forever. And when the lump gets too big you die. That's what some kids say, anyway."

Sammy nodded. "I know," she said. "Could I have yours, then—when you're done chewin' it?"

Cat was horrified. "Ugh," she said. She was about to start in on how unsanitary it was to chew other people's used gum when she remembered the other stick. Taking it out of her sweater pocket she handed it to Sammy.

It was a long time before they got back to the subject under discussion because it took Sammy practically forever to unwrap the stick of gum—without tearing the wrappers even a little—and then to bite off little tiny pieces, chewing slowly and solemnly between each bite. Cat had to repeat the question about the city of Austin three times before she got her mind far enough off the gum to answer.

Then she shook her head. "No. Not Austin," she said. "I never heerd tell 'bout no Austin."

"Where *did* you live, then?"

Sammy tipped her head thoughtfully. "On the farm," she said. "On my pa's farm."

"Okay," Cat said patiently. "You lived on your pa's farm. And when you went to town, where was that?"

The light dawned. "Ohhh!" she said. "Perryton. Town was Perryton. We used to ride to Perryton in the Studebaker. Sometimes we'd all git in the Studebaker and Pa would drive us up to Perryton to buy things."

Cat was impressed. "Oh, yeah? My brother says Studebakers are swell cars. Better than Model T's, anyways. Do your folks still have the Studebaker?"

Sammy nodded. "Course we do. Roddy and Spence sleeps in the backseat and Zane sleeps in front. Zane gets to sleep in the front seat all by hisself."

Cat was puzzled, picturing long, lanky Zane stretched out across the front seat while . . . "But how can your pa drive when Zane is sleeping in the front seat?" she asked.

Sammy seemed surprised that Cat didn't understand. "Oh, Pa don't drive the Studebaker no more," she said. "The drivin' part busted. But the sleepin' part's jist fine."

Cat was still mulling over that interesting bit of information when Sammy asked, "You want I should tell you 'bout our house—back in Texas?"

"Sure," Cat said. "Tell me about it."

Sammy's chin went up and her eyes got a faraway look. "It had a big ol' kitchen with a great big black stove—and two bedrooms and 'nother room jist for sittin' in. And out front there was this here great big stoop with a rockin' chair where Grandpa used to sit—afore he died. And there was a tree out front, too, and flowers by the fence. Lots of pretty flowers—till the dust started comin', anyways."

"The dust?" Cat asked.

Sammy's eyes went faraway again but now they seemed

wide, not with dreams, but with memories of something strange and awful. She took a long, shuddery breath before she nodded slowly and whispered, "Dust."

Cat was just about to ask Sammy to tell her more about the dust when a voice said, "Thought I'd find y'all here. Both of y'all."

And there he was, standing in the doorway. Zane Perkins.

SEVENTEEN

Zane was wearing the outgrown overalls again. The ones with the faded blue and white stripes and big holes in both knees. He was barefoot as usual and, also as usual, one side of his wide mouth was curled up in a smile that looked a lot like a sneer. Cat and Sammy were still sitting side by side on the rock shelf, and for the longest time Zane just stood there in the doorway staring at them with that mocking grin spread across one side of his face. Finally he nodded his head slowly, rolling out his lower lip like someone thinking, *Yeah, I got it*. Then he said, "Guess you two little gals been playing doll babies, huh?"

Cat slid down off the ledge. "I wasn't playing *anything*," she said. "We were just talking. And what are you doing here? I thought you said"—Cat put on a deeper voice and a real smart-alecky expression—" 'We got no interest in coming back here no more.' Didn't I hear you say something like that?"

Zane went on leaning against the door frame. "Yeah," he said in a sarcastic tone of voice, "I said that, didn't I? Jist goes to show you how things change, don't it? 'Cause, as you might could have noticed, I got me a little *interest* right there on that shelf, name of Sammy Perkins. When I

89

got home today Sammy was missin' agin and I was right *interested* in findin' out where she'd got to."

Cat pushed past him and out the door of the cottage. "Yeah, sure," she said over her shoulder. "So now you got an excuse to come here anytime Sammy's missing, huh?" She marched to the back of the grotto and, ignoring Zane completely, began straightening up the books on the high rock shelf. But he followed her and, just as if she'd invited him to, he reached up and took down one of her favorites, *Smoky the Cow Horse*. She glared at him but he pretended to be too interested in the book to notice. After a while he turned toward her.

Pointing to a picture he said, "This here Will James feller draws right good, don't he? My ma took this here book out of the liberry at Perryton onced. She used to read lots of books like this. 'Bout ranchin' and cowboys and stuff like that. Read lots of books by a feller named Grey. Zane Grey. She really liked his writin'. You heerd tell of Zane Grey?"

"Sure, I've heard of Zane Grey. He's a real famous writer. Cliff—Cliff's my brother—he reads Zane Grey a lot." Suddenly getting the connection, she was about to ask him if he'd been named after the author, when Sammy suddenly appeared in the cottage door. Still holding Marianne-Lillybelle, she stood there for a moment watching Cat and Zane anxiously. Cat watched her, and out of the corner of her eye she watched Zane as well, and for the first time noticed that he *could* smile almost like a normal person when he wanted to.

After Sammy had disappeared back inside the cottage he went back to leafing through *Smoky the Cow Horse*. Still looking at the book he said, "What was you and Sammy talkin' 'bout in there 'fore I came?"

Cat eyed him warily, wondering what he was up to now. "Well," she said, "mostly she was telling me about your farm back in Texas and how you're going to go back there someday."

Zane made a snorting noise. "Might a known it," he said. "She allays carryin' on about goin' back to our farm. And our house. She talk about goin' back to our house?"

Cat nodded and Zane shook his head, biting his lip. "Dumb kid," he said.

"Dumb?" Cat said indignantly. "I think she's real smart for a five-year-old. And besides, that's no way to talk about your own sister."

He laughed. "Look who's tellin' me how to treat Sammy —after you half scared her to death t'other day yellin' how you was goin' to sic the sheriff on her." While Cat was still trying to think of a good answer he shrugged and went on. "Thing is, she knows we ain't ever goin' back to our farm. Heck, she knows it ain't even there no more."

"The house isn't there?" Cat asked.

"Right," Zane said. "The house and the farm too. They tractored our house down right there in front of us the day we was leavin'. Saw them do it. Sammy saw them too."

"Tractored?"

"Sure." Zane was grinning again, but this time his smile wasn't devilish or friendly, either, or anything else that a smile ought to be. "After the bank foreclosed us they sent out their big ol' tractor and jist pushed our house flat over. Smashed it all to pieces. All—to—pieces," he said again, and somehow the nothing smile made Cat see it as clear as if she were watching it in a movie. This enormous roaring, smoking machine smashing the Perkinses' house while they all stood there watching. Watching it crush the kitchen and the room for sittin' in that Sammy had told about, and the big front stoop—and the rocking chair. But Zane was still talking.

"And the farm's gone too."

"How could the farm be gone?" Cat asked. "Somebody else owns it maybe, but it's still there. Farms don't go anyplace."

"They shorely do. In Texas they do nowadays, and in Oklahoma and Arkansas too. They just up and blow clean away."

She understood then. "Oh," she said, "the dust." She'd read about the Dust Bowl, of course, and she'd even seen pictures of it once in a newsreel. About how the drought and the high winds caused the earth to dry up and be carried away, covering everything in its path with a heavy, dark red dust. Picturing it and at the same time picturing the way Sammy had looked when she whispered the word *dust*, Cat's throat began the soft, swollen ache that made it hard to talk. She had to swallow hard twice before she could say, "That's awful. That must have been awful. Standing right there watching while they smashed your house. And all that dust and everything dead and—"

"Hey," Zane said. His eyes were fierce again and the hard, ornery grin was back in place, wider than ever. "Twarn't so bad. Not much worse than this ol' depression here in California, when you come right down to it. Like your pa, for instance. I'll bet your pa ain't doing so well

92

nowadays in that big old store of his'n. Don't see many people in there buying stuff, leastways not when I been in there."

A rush of anger made Cat's cheeks burn, and the soft ache in her throat was gone in an instant. "There's nothing wrong with my father's store . . ." she started, and then decided not to go on. Not to even try to argue with a stupid Okie who didn't know anything about her father's store or the Kinsey family and how they'd been in Brownwood practically forever and how they knew everyone and everyone knew them.

"Look," she said, "I don't know what you're mad about but . . ." She did know, though. All of a sudden, just as she was saying she didn't, she suddenly knew he was angry because he thought she was feeling sorry for him. And she guessed maybe she had been, just for a minute. But that didn't give him the right to say insulting things about her family. She shrugged. "Why don't you just get out of here," she said. "Go on. Get out. Right this minute."

Zane laughed. Just stood there laughing right in Cat's face for a few seconds before he turned away and walked slowly to the cottage. From where she was standing at the back of the grotto, Cat could hear him talking to Sammy. Arguing, it sounded like. At one point she clearly heard Sammy say, "Wait a minute. You wait a gol-durned minute, Zane Perkins. I got to tell her good-bye 'fore I go. I got to."

When they came out a few moments later Cat was pretending to be busy reading *Smoky the Cow Horse*. Zane had hold of Sammy's wrist, hurrying her so she had to trot to keep up.

"Stop pullin' on me," Sammy was whining. "Stop it." Digging in her heels, she was trying to jerk away when she suddenly gasped and started choking.

"Sammy? You all right?" Zane was bending over Sammy, who was still coughing, clutching her mouth with both hands. "What's the matter, Sammy?"

The coughing finally stopped, and taking her hands away from her mouth, Sammy chewed thoughtfully once or twice and then glared at her brother. "You dumb cootie," she said with her funny baby-face screwed up into an angry-cat scowl. "You jist 'bout made me swaller my gum."

"Gum?" Zane stared first at Sammy, then at Cat, and back again to Sammy. "Where'd you get gum?" he asked.

Sammy pointed. "She gived it to me. She gived it to me brand new. All wrapped up in two papers." She pulled the carefully folded gum wrappers out of her pocket and held them out for Zane to see.

Zane looked at Cat. His eyes had gone fierce again. "Don't you go givin' her stuff," he said. "She don't need folks givin' her stuff." Then he took hold of Sammy by both arms. "Spit 'er out," he demanded. "You spit out that gum, right this minute."

There was something in Zane's voice that shocked Cat and it must have shocked Sammy, too, because she didn't argue. She did cry, though. She was sobbing as she spit out the gum and then turned away toward the tunnel. Cat ran after them.

"Sammy," she called, "come back here a minute. I want to talk to you."

Sammy looked back, still sobbing. For a minute she looked from Zane to Cat and back again uncertainly, but when Zane turned loose of her shoulder she came slowly back to where Cat had stopped at the edge of the grotto.

Cupping both hands around Sammy's ear Cat whispered, "I'm going to be here again on Sunday. Sunday afternoon. Can you come too?"

Tears still dripping down her face, Sammy stared up at Cat. She caught her breath in a series of jerky little gasps, like the Model A's motor trying to start, only not as loud. She wiped her eyes with both hands and her lips curved up briefly in a wobbly smile before she nodded. A weak nod first, but then a firm, determined one.

"For sure?" Cat asked.

Sammy nodded again.

EIGHTEEN

Sunday morning was cold and cloudy and all through church Cat worried about rain. It was past the usual time for the beginning of the fall rainy season and a big downpour was probably overdue. But by the time church and Sunday dinner were over, the skies had partly cleared and it seemed a bit warmer. Much relieved, Cat waited only until Cliff took off for town and the rest of the family had settled down to their Sunday-afternoon reading and naps. Then she asked Father if she could go out to play and when he said yes she headed for the kitchen. She got the paper bag she'd packed early that morning from its hiding place in the pantry and took off running. But when she arrived at the grotto Sammy wasn't there.

She'd show up, though, Cat would bet a nickel on it. She smiled, remembering Sammy's determined nod. She felt certain that Samantha Perkins could be a pretty bullheaded little kid when she needed to be. And she probably needed to be a lot, considering the three older brothers she had to put up with. She'll be here sooner or later, Cat told herself.

After checking all around to see if everything was in

place and undisturbed, Cat went into the cottage and began unloading the bag. The dress was on top.

The dress, a pale blue cotton with little white flowers, had been sent to Cat on her sixth birthday by an aunt who lived in Iowa. But Aunt Edna, who hadn't seen Cat since she was a baby, had made the pretty little dress way too small, which was the reason it wasn't as worn and faded as most of the outgrown things in the attic. Cat spread the dress out neatly on the ledge and went back to unloading.

She took out the bananas, the sandwiches, and the cookies and arranged them on the table. At the bottom of the bag was the Kewpie doll and the celluloid dog. The Kewpie doll was about two inches high and was made of china. It had a painted-on pink-cheeked face and a fat yellow curl of china hair on top of its big round head. Cat had won it years before at a birthday party, but she'd never been especially fond of Kewpie dolls. The dog wasn't anything special either. Just a cheap little celluloid toy that looked a little bit like a cocker spaniel if you didn't look too closely. She put the two little toys next to the food on Sammy's side of the table and sat down on the ledge to wait. Sure enough, it wasn't very long before the door screeched open and Sammy came in.

As always she was barefoot and wearing the tattered remains of overalls, and no coat or sweater in spite of the cold weather. But her face was cleaner than usual and her hair seemed to have been combed sometime in the fairly recent past. When Cat said hello she ducked her head, looked up from the tops of her eyes, and whispered, "Howdy." Then her smile got braver and she said, "Howdy, Cateren."

"Cat," Cat said. "People just call me Cat."

"Oh." She looked surprised. "Zane says your school name is Cateren."

"Catherine, my real name is Catherine, but I like Cat better. Okay?"

Sammy didn't answer. She'd been edging toward the table and now that she was close enough to see, she seemed to have lost track of the conversation entirely. Looking up at Cat she swallowed hard and wiped her hand across her mouth before she said, "You fixin' to have sumpin' to eat?"

"Just a little picnic," Cat said. "I thought it might be fun to have a picnic. Don't you?"

Sammy swallowed again. "Me?" she said. "Me too?" And when Cat nodded she immediately started climbing into one of the chairs. Cat didn't eat much. Actually, she'd had Sunday dinner, the biggest meal of the whole week, not too long before and she wasn't very hungry. So she mostly just picked at the food—and watched Sammy.

Sammy loved the bananas. "I had a nanner once afore," she said in between bites. "When we-uns first got to California a man at a gas station gived me one. Only, Roddy et most of it. The man gived it to me but Roddy et most of it."

But she didn't seem to like the chicken sandwich, at least not the chicken part. When Cat put one in front of her she opened it up and stared at the meat for a minute before she put it back together and took a tiny bite. She chewed slowly with a sick look on her face and then put the sandwich back on the paper.

"Don't you like chicken?" Cat asked.

"Chicken?" Sammy asked. "Not jackrabbit? Tastes like ol' jackrabbit to me."

"You don't like rabbit?"

Sammy shook her head hard. "Back home, after the dust started, we et nothing but jackrabbit sometimes. Jist jackrabbit for days and days. And then when my pa ran out of bullets they et—Hoppy." Sammy's face had its angry cat look again. "I didn't. I wouldn't eat him but the rest of 'em did." She was breathing hard, eyes narrowed and lips puckered in a kind of baby-faced fury. "I purely hate eatin' rabbit," she whispered.

It took quite a bit more convincing before she would eat the sandwich and even then she picked out most of the chicken and gave it to Cat.

Sammy didn't seem to even notice the Kewpie doll and the celluloid dog until the food was gone. She picked them up then, one at a time, looked at them, and put them back on the table. Cat could tell she didn't imagine they were for her, but when she noticed the dress on the ledge she seemed close to guessing right away. Sliding down off the chair she went over to the ledge and, standing on tiptoes, ran her fingers around the collar and over the small blue buttons. Then she looked back at Cat questioningly.

"You goin' ter wear this here dress?" she asked.

Cat shook her head.

Sammy nodded. "Too little," she agreed. She looked down at Marianne-Lillybelle in her crib. "Too big?" she asked.

Cat nodded.

Sammy took the dress off the ledge and held it up in front of her and when Cat smiled and nodded, her face lit up in the Shirley Temple smile. In a minute she had stripped down to a pair of flour-sack underpants and was pulling the blue dress over her head. But while she was carefully buttoning the flower-shaped buttons and backing up for Cat to tie the sash, Cat kept seeing something else—the pale blue-white skin and sharply defined ribs of Sammy's skinny little body.

"Wished I had me a lookin' glass," Sammy was saying, looking down at herself and running her hands down her front and then out to the side to pull the full skirt out into a half circle. Then she started parading around, twirling now and then to make the skirt stand out and twisting to see herself from every angle. She looked absolutely thrilled and delighted—but cold.

Cat worried about the cold. The overalls and shirt had been little enough, but the short-sleeved, summery dress was even worse, and when she tried to get Sammy to put the shirt on over the dress she refused.

"Raggedy old thing," she said, pushing it away, and when Cat insisted she said, "In a minute. I got to go home in a minute, anyways. Afore they all gets back from work."

"Before who gets home from work?" Cat asked.

"All of 'em."

"On Sunday? And your brothers too? They're all working on Sunday?"

Sammy nodded absently, still admiring herself. "Till the grapes are done. Mr. Otis got to get the grapes in afore the rain gets bad. So everybody has to work, 'cept me." Sammy twirled one last time before she went to the window, looked out, sighed, and then began to unbutton the dress. "I got to go now," she said.

When she was back in her shirt and overalls, she folded the dress carefully and put it back on the ledge. Then she hurriedly thanked Cat for the picnic and, looking anxious and worried, started for the door.

"Wait a minute," Cat said. "You can take the dress with you. And those things on the table too. I brought them for you."

Sammy came back. She picked up the Kewpie doll and the dog and examined each one carefully as if for the first time. Then she went back to the dress. Running her fingers over the fancy buttons she looked at it longingly before she turned to Cat with what might have seemed like a cheerful smile if you didn't look at her eyes.

"I think I'd jist as lief save it for when I'm here," she said. "For when I comes here agin to visit. And them toys too."

Cat frowned. "But I wanted you to take them home," she said. "Why can't you take the dress home?" She thought she knew the answer but she wanted to see what Sammy would say.

"Cause I got to be a boy till we gets back to Texas," she said firmly.

"And the toys? Why can't you take the toys?"

Sammy rolled her eyes thoughtfully. "Roddy would break 'em?" she said in a questioning tone, as if she were asking Cat if she'd go for that explanation. And when Cat pursed her lips skeptically, she added, "And 'cause of Zane. Zane don't like folks givin' us stuff. Zane don't like us to be beggin' like."

Cat thought so. She shrugged impatiently. "Well, I don't see why you have to do everything Zane tells you to do," she said.

Sammy nodded uncertainly. Then she stuck out her chin and nodded more firmly. Going back to the table she picked up the Kewpie doll and tried to put it in her overall pocket, but it was a little too big. The celluloid dog fit fine. "I'll take this here one," she said, patting her pocket triumphantly. Then she threw her arms around Cat's middle, gave her a quick hug, and ran out the door.

Cat sat down on the ledge and stayed there, just thinking, for a long time. She thought mostly about Sammy. Almost entirely about Sammy. She went on thinking about her most of the way home. It wasn't until she was crossing the empty pasture behind the Kinsey house that she remembered the reason she'd taken all those things to the grotto in the first place. Right at first she'd mostly been thinking about paying Zane back. Paying him back for being too mean to let his little sister have a measly old stick of chewing gum, just because someone gave it to her.

At least that had been the reason in the beginning. It was funny how she'd almost forgotten about paying Zane back.

NINETEEN

Cat was sure, pretty sure at least, that Sammy had kept their Sunday meeting a secret. Or maybe not—because Zane was obviously angry about something. Either he thought he had something to be mad about, or else he was just naturally getting meaner all the time. Because all that next week at school it seemed as if he was trying his best to make Cat's life as miserable as possible.

For one thing he had suddenly started joining in when people pestered her about racing with him. "Come on, Cat Kinsey," he started saying. "Let's you and me have a little ol' race." And of course everyone else would chime in. "Yeah, Cat. Come on. Why don't you race with the fast Okie? Be a good sport, Cat."

And then Zane would say, "Yeah, Cat. How's about it? Be a good sport." That made her madder than anything—when Zane Perkins called her Cat, like they were old friends, and told her to be a good sport.

And when Zane wasn't tormenting her about racing with him, he was apt to be hanging around looking at her. When she took her turn on the bars he usually just stood there watching, but once or twice when her skirt came untucked from the legs of her underpants he joined right in with the other boys who liked to say nasty things like "I see London, I see France. I see someone's underpants."

He also started making a nuisance of himself when she was trying to beat her record on Janet's new paddleball—a fancy twenty-five-cent one that had a nice thick paddle with a special coating to made it less slippery.

Cat was almost as good at paddleball as she was at running and she'd kept the ball going once for almost five hundred strokes, which would have been a new Brownwood record. She'd have broken the record easy if Janet hadn't gotten so excited she started jumping up and down and squealing, which ruined Cat's concentration and made her miss. But recently she hadn't been able to get anywhere near five hundred because of Zane. It was hard to keep her mind on hitting the ball squarely and counting the strokes when she knew he was staring at her, just trying to make her miss. Watching and counting out loud in his dumb Okie accent. Saying things like "tyou" when he meant two and "fahve" instead of five.

Usually she simply tried to ignore him, but once in a while she'd get so fed up, she'd turn around and stare back. And then he'd just grin and pretend he was looking at something else.

It was rainy on Wednesday and again on Thursday, and having to stay indoors every recess gave Zane Perkins a lot of new opportunities to make a nuisance of himself. Like for instance choosing *Cat's pigtail* to be the answer in a game of twenty questions. Cat hated for anyone to call her braid a pigtail and she hated it even more when Zane did it. But the worst thing of all happened when they were playing musical chairs. Just as Miss Albright stopped the music, Zane pushed his way into a chair that Cat was headed for, so that just for a moment she was sitting in his lap. Of course everyone had to tease her about that all the rest of the day.

By Friday the rain had stopped but Zane's pestering didn't let up. It was during the noon recess on Friday, when Cat was playing dodgeball, that she fell down and skinned both her knees, and it was Zane Perkins's fault.

The game had just started and there were a lot of dodgers still in the circle. Hank Belton was on the outside team. Hank was a good thrower and when he played dodgeball he threw hard and fast—and usually right at Cat. So this one time when Hank got the ball he wound up like crazy and threw at Cat, and just as she started to dodge Zane Perkins jumped right in between her and the ball. The ball missed Cat and hit Zane, but Cat hit Zane too. Ran right into him in midjump and crashed down on the blacktop and skinned both her knees.

It hurt a lot, but if there were tears in her eyes when she got to her feet it was mostly from anger. She pushed aside the hands that were trying to help her up and stormed off to the office, where Mrs. Jayne, the principal, kept her first-aid kid.

Mrs. Jayne was not very sympathetic. "Not again!" she said when Cat limped into her room. "You're just going to have to slow down a little, child. I never in my life knew anyone with such a full-tilt-ahead approach to life. You're not going to have any knees left if you keep this up."

Cat didn't appreciate the lecture, particularly since this time the skinned knees weren't her fault. But she didn't say anything. She wasn't going to be a snitch, not even about an Okie. But at least being angry helped her to keep from crying when Mrs. Jayne dabbed on the iodine.

A few minutes later when she was on her way back down the hall, with her knees hurting worse than ever from the iodine, she passed Spence Perkins, sitting on the railing as usual.

"Wooee!" Spence said as she went by. "That must be ahurtin' some," and there was something in the way he said it that made her stop and look at him. He looked and sounded so much like Zane—but with a mysterious difference that she couldn't quite put her finger on. He was younger, of course, eight or nine instead of twelve, but there was more to it than that. For one thing he certainly seemed friendlier and a little less ornery. Cat decided to sit down on the railing for a minute until her knees stopped hurting.

Pausing every few seconds to blow on her knees, she said, "How do you—and your brothers—like Brownwood School, now that you've been here awhile?"

Spence nodded slowly, smiling with that same wide Perkins mouth—*but* with the mysterious difference. "Jist fine," he said. "Leastways a lot better than the last place we tried to go to school."

"Where was that?"

"Down south a ways. Town name of Cottonville."

Cat was intrigued. She'd hadn't expected him to say they liked it at Brownwood. How could they when everybody, or nearly everybody, called them Okies, and made fun of their accents and bare feet and raggedy clothing? "What happened at Cottonville?" she asked.

He shrugged. "Teachers made us sit on the floor at the

back of the room. And some of 'em wouldn't let us have books, nor paper and pencils even. This one teacher wouldn't even call any of us camp kids by our rightful names. Jist pointed and said, 'Okie. Hey you, Okie.' "

It was a peculiar thing. Listening to Spence's soft, shy voice, Cat kept on hearing the difference and guessing how Zane would have told about Cottonville. It would have been, she guessed, with the same shocking fierceness that had been there when he made Sammy spit out the gum. But Spence didn't sound fierce or angry at all when he said *Okie*.

She turned away, embarrassed by the hurt on Spence's face, and when she looked back he was sitting quietly, looking down at his hands. For no reason at all Cat suddenly felt guilty—and angry that he'd made her feel that way. She'd always hated it when people made her feel guilty.

"Well, people call you Okies here too," she said. "And that's what you are, aren't you?"

She'd meant to make him mad but when he looked up he was smiling. "No siree," he said. "Not us Perkinses, anyways. We're from Texas. From Panhandle country right 'nough, but 'cross the border in Texas. So we're Texans, not Okies."

"I know that," Cat said impatiently. "But when people say *Okie* they don't just mean people from Oklahoma."

Spence laughed shortly. "You're shorely right 'bout that," he said. "When Californians say *Okie* they mean *dumb* and *dirty* and *lazy* and most everthin' else bad they can think of."

It was true, of course. Cat wanted to say it wasn't but she couldn't bring herself to do it. It would be too much of a lie. Trying to change the subject—just for something to say—she asked, "How's Sammy?"

Spence sighed and shook his head. "Sammy's sick," he said.

"Sick?" It was like a squeezing hand had caught at something in Cat's chest. "What's the matter with her?"

"Don't know for sure," Spence said. "But it might could be her lungs agin. Back in Texas she had dust-lung real bad jist 'fore we left."

"Dust lung?" Cat's hand went to her chest and she breathed deeply, feeling a sort of dry stiffness there, just from imagining what "dust lung" must be like. Then, remembering Granny Cooper and her long naps, she asked, "Well, who's looking out for her? Who's seeing that she doesn't go wandering around in the cold making herself worse?"

"Ma is," Spence said. "Ma stayed home from work yesterday and today too. She's fixin' to work tomorrow, though, lessen Sammy's worse."

Cat nodded and sat for a while thinking. Then she got down off the railing gingerly. Her knees weren't hurting quite as badly, but they'd started to stiffen up a little. She shook one leg and then the other before she asked, casually, as if for no particular reason, "All you folks going to be working again this weekend?"

"Yep," Spence said. "All of us 'ceptin' Sammy. And Ma, maybe, if Sammy's real bad in the mornin'."

Cat said, "Well, good-bye. I got to go now." She limped off down the hall thinking about Sammy and making plans. Planning a visit—to the grotto first—and then maybe on down to . . . She couldn't believe she was actually thinking of visiting Okietown—but she was.

TWENTY

On Saturday morning Mama had one of her sick headaches. As soon as the others left for the store, she went back to bed. Cat pulled down the blinds in Mama's room and brought her some aspirins, a glass of water, and a wet washcloth. She waved the washcloth in the air to make it nice and cool and then arranged it carefully on Mama's forehead. Mama opened her eyes, smiled weakly, and patted Cat's hand.

"You're being very kind and thoughtful today," she said. "You're a good daughter, Cathy." Cat wanted to jerk her hand away angrily but she didn't. The anger was because Mama was being helpless and pitiful as usual, and making Cat feel guilty. Even more guilty than usual this time because, down deep, she'd been at least a little bit glad when Mama said she was getting sick. Not because Mama's head was aching, of course, but a little bit glad that now she'd sleep most of the day, which would leave Cat free to do whatever she wanted.

It was probably because of the guilty feeling that Cat stood there by Mama's bed for quite a while asking her if she wanted some more aspirin, or a piece of ice, or a different pillow.

"Or I could call Dr. Wilson," Cat said. "Would you like me to call Dr. Wilson?"

"No," Mama said, in her weak headachy voice. "There's nothing anyone can do for my headaches, I'm afraid. Not even the famous Dr. Wilson."

Mama wasn't being sarcastic. Dr. Wilson, a big round-faced man with a slow, gentle voice, was practically famous, at least in Brownwood. He was particularly famous for curing people with serious diseases like bronchitis or pneumonia. Ellen was always wishing out loud that Dr. Wilson had been their doctor when her mother had pneumonia. Ellen always sighed wistfully when she said that, to show how much she wished her mother were still alive.

"Oh, if only Dr. Wilson had been in Brownwood back then, Mother would still be alive today," Ellen would say. And there was always something about the way she looked right at Cat that seemed to add something more. Something about the fact that Cat would never have been born if Eleanor were still alive—and Ellen made it pretty plain she didn't think that would be so bad either.

But Mama didn't want Dr. Wilson to come. So Cat brought more water, and then sat there in the room and waited until the sound of Mama's breathing became deep and even. Then she tiptoed out the door and down the hall.

Less than a minute later she was shrugging into her coat and heading for the back door. Partway across the kitchen she stopped, went back to her room, and pawed through the closet until she found what she was looking for—a sweater that she'd had for years but never worn very much. An old rose-colored sweater that Ellen had made when she was just learning to knit. It was a little bit lopsided, with one sleeve longer than the other, but it was heavy and warm and not very worn out. After tying it around her waist under the coat, Cat again tiptoed down the hall. When the back door closed behind her she began to run.

It wasn't raining but it was another cold, gray day. The heavy rains on Wednesday and Thursday had left the air damp and clammy and mud puddles were everywhere. In the canyon the muddy water of the creek was higher, and parts of Cat's favorite paths were flooded. Detours around or over boulders were necessary, and now and then daring crossings of flooded areas by jumping from stone to stone. By the time she reached the grotto she was sweating in spite of the cold air.

The little sandy strip in front of the blackberry thicket was quite a bit narrower, and the air in the tunnel smelled damp and earthy. Inside the grotto, however, everything was dry, protected from the rain by the rocky overhang, and from the flooding by the slight rise of the grotto floor. All Cat's belongings were safe and in their proper places—and no one was in the cottage.

She hadn't really expected Sammy to be there, but she had to be sure. If Mrs. Perkins had gone back to work today, as Spence said she might, and if Granny Cooper's napping habits hadn't changed, there was no telling what a headstrong and determined kid like Sammy might do, if she wanted to badly enough. Even a little kid who had just been sick. And if Sammy Perkins wanted to do anything really badly, it might very well be to visit the grotto—and Lillybelle.

But Sammy wasn't in the cottage and probably hadn't been there since last Sunday. The Kewpie doll and Lillybelle were exactly where they had been, and the blue dress was still lying on the ledge, just the way Sammy had left it.

Cat took the sweater out from under her coat, folded it carefully, and put it on top of the dress. For Sammy's next visit. She'd been thinking of Sammy playing in the cottage, wearing the thick, warm sweater over the pretty blue dress. But on further consideration she had to admit that Sammy probably shouldn't visit the grotto again anytime soon. Not in this cold, rainy weather and with the creek on the rise.

Of course, there probably wasn't much point in taking the sweater to Sammy at home. Certainly not if Zane was around, at least. But because she couldn't decide what else to do, Cat tied the sweater back around her waist by its lopsided sleeves before she crawled back through the tunnel.

Downstream from the grotto the creekside paths were flooded in places just as they had been farther up the canyon. As Cat headed downstream toward Okietown, picking her way carefully over muddy stretches and around boulders, she tried not to think about all the terrible things she'd heard about the Okie camps. All the stories about dirt and disease and mean, sneaky people who'd just as soon stick a knife in you as look at you.

Trying to keep from worrying, she told herself that, according to what Spence had said, almost all of the grownups would surely be away at work. But then a sneaky little interior voice added, *All except for the really bad ones who probably never work anyway. Never work, and just hang around the camp instead, waiting for somebody to come along they could stick a knife into.* Two or three times, imagining all the

112

awful people she might meet and the terrible things that might happen to her, she stopped and turned back toward home. But each time she went on again.

She stopped again for a longer time when she reached the wooded hillside from which it was possible to look right down into Okietown. It wasn't really a town at all, of course. Except for four tiny wooden shacks that Mr. Otis had built years before to house some of his ranch hands, there were no real buildings at all. Just a collection of tents and lean-to sheds built of what seemed to be cardboard and canvas and pieces of rusty corrugated tin.

Among the tents and shacks were piles of trash where scraps of cardboard, tin, and glass mingled with the remains of dead cars. Oily pipes and wires, looking like metal veins and intestines, made ugly clumps among other broken body parts, such as bumpers, fenders, and running boards. Cat shuddered.

When she'd stood on that exact same spot a few weeks before, looking down on Okietown, everything had been covered by a gray veil of dust. The gray was gone now, but in its place were other ugly colors—muddy browns, dark red rusts like streaks of dried blood, and the nameless shades of rain-wet canvas and soggy cardboard.

No one was in sight. Maybe they *were* all away working. All except Granny Cooper and Sammy, at least. Cat squared her shoulders, raised her chin, and started down the hill.

On the outskirts of the camp she passed what was obviously an outhouse, a tiny enclosure made of an old billboard advertising Wonder Bread. The door was a sagging curtain of ragged gunnysacks. Cat walked faster, holding her breath against the smell. She was still hurrying when she rounded the first shack and nearly walked right over two little kids.

The children were squatting beside a deep puddle, doing something with a tin can and a stick. Still squatting, they stared up at Cat, their faces stiff with mud and surprise.

Cat tried to smile. "Hello," she said. "I'm looking for the Perkinses'. . ." She discarded *house* and *home* and wound up with *place*. "I'm looking for the Perkinses' place. Do you know where the Perkinses live?"

For a moment no one spoke and it didn't look like they were going to. The littlest kid, in fact, stuck a muddy thumb into his mouth like a cork and kept it there. But at last the other one, a pale, pointy-faced little boy with no-color hair, raised one arm and pointed to a tent only a few yards away.

Cat pointed too. "There?" she asked. "Is that it?" and the gray-faced boy nodded silently. Cat said thank you, carefully walked around the kids and their mudhole, and made her way down the soggy road.

The Perkinses' place was not exactly a shack or completely a tent. A canvas roof and walls had been hung over a rough wooden frame. On one side the canvas wall had been pulled out and draped over a car, an old rusty Studebaker that sat deep in the muddy earth on bare wheel-rims.

A front section of the tent had been tied back so it was possible to see most of what was inside. At the rear of the dark enclosure Cat could just make out a small stove made of what seemed to be heavy tin. There were no chairs or tables. Two mattresses, a wide one and another cot sized, covered most of the floor. On some shelves against the right wall she could make out a washboard, a few pots, several jars, a few pieces of cracked pottery, and a familiar object—a small pail made from an oilcan with a bailing-wire handle.

There was no color anywhere. Everything, the tent walls, the blankets covering the mattresses, even the things in the cupboard, seemed faded and soiled to a dull gray sameness. Everything, that is, except for the flower on the orange crate that sat beside the entrance to the tent.

Someone had planted the flower, a geranium, in a rusty tin can. It was a scrawny, crooked plant but its blossoms, a bright orangish red, stood out bravely against the colorless tent wall. Cat was staring at the geranium when, out of the corner of her eye, she saw something move, and there on the narrow mattress a mop of tousled hair framing a small familiar face was appearing from under a pile of dirty gray blankets.

TWENTY-ONE

"Well, hi, Sammy," Cat said, trying for a smile and tone of voice that would hide how shocked and dismayed she felt. "Spence told me you were sick, so I thought I'd just drop by for a visit."

Sammy sat up. She was wearing a nightgown that had once been a flour sack. Her face was thinner and very pale. Blue veins showed through the skin on each side of her forehead. "Cateren?" She sounded uncertain, as if she didn't believe her eyes.

Cat smiled and nodded. "That's right, Cateren," she said, imitating Sammy's pronunciation. Then she curtsied, holding her skirt out at each side, and, in a prissy, hoity-toity voice, said, "Miss Catherine Kinsey, actually. Come to call on Miss Samantha Perkins."

Sammy caught on right away. Smiling delightedly she said, "Well, come right on in, Miss Kinsey, and set awhile. Set right down here and . . ." At that point Sammy looked down at her flour-sack nightgown and seemed to lose her train of thought. Quickly wrapping herself in a ragged blanket to hide the faded letters that spelled GRANTS FLOUR MILL across her chest, she glanced up anxiously to see if Cat had noticed. But when Cat looked away, pretending to be examining her own muddy feet, Sammy quickly got back into the game. "Set down on this here . . ." she said, and then hesitated, looking around the barren tent before she went on, "right here on my bed."

But as Cat came into the tent, carefully making her way down the narrow passageway between the two mattresses, Sammy began to cough. A hard, racking cough that rasped in her throat and shook her small body fiercely. When the coughing fit finally eased Cat asked, "How're you feeling, anyway, Sammy? Spence said you were real sick. You don't have anything catching, do you? Like measles or scarlet fever?"

Still fighting the cough Sammy shook her head, tried to speak, and coughed again. Finally she managed to gasp. "No. Nuthin' like that. 'Sides, I'm better now. Tomorrow Ma's goin' to let me git up." And as Cat still hesitated she repeated, "Come on in and set."

But Cat couldn't bring herself to sit down on the dirty blankets. She was still standing awkwardly beside Sammy's bed when she remembered the orange crate. "Just a minute," she said, and ducked back out under the tent flap. Placing the geranium in its tin-can planter carefully on the ground, she carried the sturdy box into the tent. "Look," she told Sammy. "A chair. A beautiful chair. Probably an antique, don't you think?"

Sammy was coughing again but she managed a quick smile. Going back to her visiting-lady act Cat sat down primly, knees together and hands folded neatly in her lap. Sammy watched, pressing both hands to her mouth to hold back the cough.

"Yes, thank you," Cat said. "I will have a cup of tea. Lemon, please, and lots of sugar." Then she pretended to be drinking, stirring first and then holding the imaginary cup daintily, little finger extended. Sammy giggled—started to drink a pretend cup of tea herself—and began to cough again.

By the time the coughing fit finally ended Sammy had forgotten about the pretend tea party. Instead she was thinking about Lillybelle. "I was worrin' 'bout her, in the rain and all," she said. "She didn't get wet or nuthin', did she?"

"No. She's fine. I stopped in to see on my way here. Everything in the grotto is dry and Lillybelle is too." Cat paused, realizing that she, too, was calling Marianne Lillybelle. But then she shrugged and said, "Lillybelle told me to give you her love and to tell you to get well real quick."

A faint shadow of the dimple appeared in Sammy's thin cheek and her shoulders lifted in a happy shiver. "What else'd she say?" she asked. "What else'd Lillybelle tell you to tell me?"

"Well . . ." Cat was still groping for something really exciting to tell when another voice said, "Well, land sakes, if we ain't got ourselves a visitor. Sammy, baby, you didn't tell me you was expectin' somebody to come callin'."

Cat jumped to her feet. "Hello," she said. "I'm Catherine Kinsey. I came because I heard Sammy was sick. Spence told me. I go to Brownwood School and yesterday when I was talking to Spence he told me she was sick so I just decided to—to . . ." She stuttered to a stop.

The woman in the entrance of the tent was tall and thin. Her long gray-brown hair was tied back except for a few strands that straggled around her face. She was wearing a colorless cotton dress and a torn and raveled sweater that might once have been bright blue. She put down a lard-can pail full of water and came into the tent.

"That was right neighborly of you," she told Cat. "Right neighborly. Must not have been too easy getting way out here in all this mud. Road out to the highway is jist a bunch of mudholes."

Cat thought of mentioning that she'd come down the canyon, and decided against it. "Yes, it was pretty muddy," she said.

There was an uncomfortable silence and then Mrs. Perkins said, "You say you're in Spence's class?"

Cat was used to people taking her to be younger than she was. "No," she said. "I'm in sixth grade. In Zane's class."

"Well, do tell." Mrs. Perkins put her hands on her hips. "You're a mite of a thing to be in sixth grade. In Zane's class, you say? Zane's took quite a likin' to school here in Brownwood. Don't want to miss a day. 'Most like he used to be back in Texas. Used to be right good at his school-work back in Texas. Jist like his little brother. Spence always has liked school better'n anythin'. But when we got to Californy Zane got so he wouldn't even go for a while there. Till we got here to Brownwood."

When Mrs. Perkins talked about Zane her face changed, lightening the shadows and softening the tight lines around her mouth. She was starting to say something more about him when Sammy started to cough again. Kneeling beside the bed her mother felt her forehead and wrapped the blanket more firmly around her shoulders.

"Don't you go gettin' chilled," she said. "And p'raps you'd best be lyin' down agin now, 'fore you go gettin' yourself wore out."

"I've got to be going anyway," Cat said. "I just came by for a minute to see how Sammy was getting along and—" Suddenly her hands went to her middle, where the bulky sweater was still tied around her waist. There was no use trying to give anything to Sammy now. Just like Zane, Mrs. Perkins would probably refuse to let Sammy keep anything Cat gave her. She looked at Sammy lying on the thin mattress, wrapped in the ragged blanket, and suddenly her lips tightened.

"Mrs. Perkins," she said, "I brought Sammy a present. I brought it all this way and I'd surely like her to have it." She had been untying the sweater as she was talking and now she held it out to Sammy's mother. Mrs. Perkins was frowning as she took the heavy rose-colored sweater in her scarred, work-worn hands. Cat was getting ready to argue, when Sammy said, "Ma?"

Sammy was sitting up again, holding out both arms and smiling. The blanket had fallen off and her arms were bare and very thin. Mrs. Perkins looked at Sammy and then at Cat and there was no anger in her frown, only a kind of patient sadness. Kneeling down beside the bed she pulled the warm sweater over Sammy's thin arms and down over her smiling face.

It wasn't until Cat was on her way home, climbing the first slope above Okietown, that she suddenly realized that Mrs. Perkins had accepted not only the present but something else too. Cat was certain she'd slipped up and said *she* or *her* about Sammy at least once or twice, and Mrs. Perkins hadn't said a thing. And she especially remembered that as she was saying good-bye Mrs. Perkins said, "Thanks agin for the sweater. Jist what Sammy needed in this cold weather. Looks right nice on her too."

120

Mrs. Perkins had said *her*. Cat was sure of that. So she had also accepted that Cat knew Sammy was a girl.

At the small grove of trees where she'd stood twice before looking down on Okietown, Cat stopped to rest and catch her breath. It was nearly noon now and the sun had broken through a rift in the dark clouds. In the direct sunlight Okietown looked, not brighter, but more distinct, oily blacks gleaming sharply against dirty browns and dull grays.

Now that she knew exactly where it was, Cat could easily pick out the Perkinses' place with its Studebaker bedroom and open-door flap. Feeling again the damp cold of the interior of the tent, a cold that for some reason seemed even more bone chilling than the outdoor air, Cat shuddered. She was still staring at the tent, seeing in her mind's eye the stove, the mattresses, and the wet canvas walls, when Mrs. Perkins appeared in the doorway. She was carrying the orange crate and as Cat watched she put it back where it had been just outside the entrance. Then she picked up the geranium and arranged it carefully on the box before she went back into the tent.

As Cat watched from the hillside a narrow ray of sunlight drifted over Okietown. As it passed the Perkinses' tent it turned the bright spot of orangy-red into a tiny beacon, shining briefly against the dull sameness of its surroundings. But a minute later the clouds closed in again and the geranium in its tin-can planter faded into the shadows. Cat turned and ran for home.

TWENTY-TWO

It rained again on Sunday and Monday and almost every day for the rest of that week. The hills around town were quickly changing from summer gold to winter green. The usual Brownwood winter pattern had begun, green hills, muddy roads, and little trickling creeks turning into rushing torrents. The path beside Brownwood Road had become a series of mud puddles, so that Cat, on her way to school, had to stay on the pavement. No running along the shoulder and certainly no shortcuts over the Three Sisters' Ridge.

It was that same rainy week that Cat started having long talks with Spence Perkins almost every day. It was getting to be a kind of habit. Every noon hour at about twelve forty-five Cat would leave the playground, or on rainy days her own classroom, to go to the girls' rest room. And on the way back she'd make a detour down the hall that passed by Mrs. Peters's third- and fourth-grade room, where Spence Perkins usually sat on the railing during recesses. As soon as she came around the corner Spence would look up from the book he was reading, grin, and say, "Howdy, Cat Kinsey."

And Cat would say "Howdy, Spence Perkins."

Most often they began the conversation by talking about Sammy.

Sammy was getting better. On Monday she was allowed out of bed but not yet out of the tent, Spence said.

It was on Wednesday that Cat just happened to ask, "Is your mother still staying home every day with Sammy?"

"Yeah," Spence said. "My pa too. There ain't no work to go to, noways. Crops are all done. What didn't get picked got rotted by the rain. No work around here no more." Spence ran his hand through his thick, straggly hair and looked up at Cat through narrowed eyes, as if watching for her reaction as he said, "Everybody's movin' on in a day or two. The whole camp. Soon as Mr. Otis pays up on Friday. Work ended two, three days ago, but Mr. Otis only pays on Fridays no matter what."

"Moving on? You mean your family's going away too?" Cat couldn't believe it. She felt shocked and hurt, as if she had somehow been betrayed.

Spence shrugged and nodded. "Got to," he said. "No more work around here."

"But you can't," Cat said. "I mean, you said yourself how much you all like Brownwood School. And how you're all doing so well here." Actually, she really had no way of knowing how well Spence and Roddy were doing, but she had noticed how much Zane seemed to have improved in his schoolwork. When he first came to Brownwood he'd been way behind, especially in fractions and decimals, but Miss Albright had given him lots of extra work and lately he seemed to be almost caught up.

Spence shrugged. "Yeah," he said. "But we gotta. You

gotta work or you don't eat. And there jist ain't no work around here no more." Then he grinned ruefully. "Tain't my fault, Cat Kinsey."

Cat realized then that she'd been glaring. She sighed and shrugged. "I know it!" she said crossly. "But it just doesn't seem right."

"Well, we won't be going right off, like tomorrer, or maybe even next week, like as not. Leastways us Perkinses won't. Like I tole you, Mr. Otis ain't paying everybody off till Friday and then my pa's got to get some tires and a new generator for the Studebaker. And then him and Elmer got to get it runnin' agin. And that might take 'nother three, four days."

"Elmer?" Cat asked.

"Yeah. Elmer Davis. Elmer's a friend of ours who's right good with engines."

"My brother's good with engines too," Cat said. "He's been keeping our car running for years, all by himself. My brother likes Studebakers. Does your friend Elmer like Studebakers?"

Spence smiled. "Guess so. Guess right now he'd like anythin' that would run. He ain't got no car of his own right now. So he's goin' to help Pa get the Studebaker runnin' an' then he's goin' to hitch a ride with us. Far as we're goin', anyways."

Cat had a momentary mental picture of how that would look. Three grown-ups and four kids plus mattresses, cooking utensils, washboards, and tubs, not to mention oilcan pails, all crowded in, and on top of, one beat-up old car. She'd seen them before—Okies on the road to who knows where. But she hadn't *known* any of them before.

"Where are you going, for heaven's sake?" Cat realized

her tone of voice still sounded accusing, but she couldn't seem to help it.

"Not sure for certain. Pa heerd tell that there's still work in the cotton down near Bakersfield."

"So you're just going to start out and go all that way when you don't even know for sure there'll be any work when you get there. That sounds pretty dumb to me. And when you get there you'll probably be all out of money and there won't be any work after all, most likely."

Spence nodded. "Most likely," he said meekly, agreeing with what Cat had said instead of fighting back like Zane surely would have done. She could imagine what Zane would have said if he'd been there—and the *way* he'd have said it with that one-sided curl to his lip and the hateful, teasing eyes. "Humph," Cat said, and stomped off feeling angry without knowing why. At Spence, somehow, for what he hadn't said—which didn't make much sense. And even more at Zane for what he probably would have said if he'd been there. Cat was still imagining what Zane would have said, and the way he would have said it, when she got to the classroom—and there he was sitting on her desk.

Harry Bailey, who was the best artist in the whole school, was drawing on the blackboard, cartoons of Maggie and Jiggs and the Katzenjammer Kids. A bunch of kids were watching, standing around the front of the room or sitting on top of some front-row desks. Cat's desk was in the front row and the person who was sitting on it was Zane Perkins. Just sitting there on top of *her* desk like it belonged to him. Swinging his bare feet and talking to Eddie Bonner, who was sitting on Janet's desk, just across the aisle.

Cat sat down at her desk, pulled out her big heavy geography book, and shoved it against Zane's backside as hard as she could. "Get off my desk, Zane Perkins," she said.

Zane kind of jumped, but then he turned around slowly and stared at Cat for quite a while before he said, "Well, now. Since yer askin' me so perlite like, I guess I'll have to do jist that."

Everybody laughed. And not like they were laughing at Zane either. Cat opened her geography book and pretended she was reading about the rivers of Mesopotamia, but really she was thinking how disgusting people like Eddie Bonner were. People who started liking somebody —somebody they'd had no use for not too long ago—just because they turned out to be real good at something, like running, for instance.

It wasn't until the teacher came in and everybody went back to their own seats that Cat began to really think about why she'd been so upset by what Spence had told her. Why should she care what the Perkinses did, anyway? It was none of her business, and after all, the Perkinses didn't mean anything to her except—except perhaps for Sammy. Cat thought, off and on, about Sammy that whole afternoon, and a lot more at home that evening.

When she sat by her window that night it seemed like Okietown and Sammy were just about all she could think about. It was raining again, a hard, steady downpour that seemed like it was never going to end. Listening to the rustle and rush and spatter and watching the gray ravelings of rain slanting through the light from her window, Cat felt sad and melancholy without knowing exactly why. Usually she liked the rain. Liked listening to its cold gray song while she sat safe and warm behind the windowpane. But tonight was different.

Tonight when she looked out into the wet darkness she kept seeing a pale, thin face. Sammy's face, wet with tears or rain, floating above a dark huddle of tents and shanties that seemed to be slowly collapsing into an endlessly spreading sea of cold, black mud.

It was still raining on Monday. Cat went to the girls' rest room early and she was already waiting in the hall when Spence came out of Mrs. Peters's room.

After they'd both said, "Howdy," Cat said, "Well, I see you're still here. How's the Studebaker coming along?"

Spence shrugged. "Well, they're workin' on it. Jist got it all tore up so far. But Elmer thinks they'll have it back together 'fore long."

"And running?" Cat asked.

"Well, maybe for a day or two, anyways, if we're real lucky." Spence's twisted grin was brave, Cat thought. Brave to be able to laugh about something so life-or-death important as the old Studebaker was to the Perkinses right now.

"I'll bet they get it running real soon," she said. "Cliff says Studebakers are long-lasting cars."

Spence nodded and his smile became a little less painful. "We got a house now, anyways," he said. "After the Laytons left we moved into their cabin. Ain't much of a house but it's drier and right warm when the stove's agoin'. Ma thought a warm room to sleep in might help Sammy get over her cough."

"Is she better?" Cat asked. "Is Sammy better?"

Spence looked at Cat, shrugged, and looked away. Then he turned toward the playground, where rain was still spattering on the blacktop and splashing into the small lakes that had once been sawdust pits.

Ignoring Cat's question he only said, "Shorely do wish it would stop rainin'."

TWENTY-THREE

That night Cat sat at her window for a long time. For the first time in what seemed like ages it was a clear, almost cloudless night. The man in a nearly full moon seemed to have a startled expression on his face, as if he were surprised about something. Surprised, maybe, to see that California hadn't washed completely away after all, and that it had finally come out from behind all those everlasting clouds.

Cat knew *she* was certainly glad to see an end to the rain. Calm, clear nights with lots of moonlight sometimes gave her a hopeful feeling. And right now something, perhaps the moonlight, was making her feel that all sorts of problems could be solved if only people would get to know each other instead of being so suspicious and frightened just because of a few differences. If they'd just get acquainted, for instance, the way she'd gotten to know Sammy and Spence—and Mrs. Perkins too. And Zane? She wasn't including Zane. At least not very much.

She'd been thinking about the Perkinses and their problems for a while when she suddenly came up with a wonderful plan. The plan was to find Mr. Perkins a job in

Brownwood so Sammy and, of course, all the other Perkinses, too, wouldn't have to move away.

She knew, of course, how scarce jobs were nowadays with the depression and all. And how even people like Cliff had tried for months and months to find work without any luck. But that was different. That wouldn't be the same at all because Cliff had been looking for a different kind of work. Cliff, who had not only a high school diploma but also two years at the junior college, had been looking for a job as a salesman or in an office. And Mr. Perkins would probably want to do farming work or at least something where he didn't have to sit in an office or wear a coat and tie. And, it suddenly occurred to Cat, she knew where just that kind of job could be found. Right in Kinsey's Hardware. Mr. Perkins could take over Ernie's old job in the stockroom of Kinsey's Hardware.

It wasn't the kind of job where you needed to have a lot of special training or education. Or the kind of clothes people had to wear if they worked out in front and had to meet the public a lot. Ernie hadn't much education at all, but for years and years he'd taken care of loading and unloading and keeping things neat and orderly in the stockroom. And in the evenings after closing he'd swept and dusted and stocked the shelves in the front of the store. But then a few years ago Ernie had gone off to an old folks' home and Father just hadn't yet hired someone to take his place. Instead he and Cliff and sometimes even Ellen had been taking turns doing Ernie's work. Not that Cliff and Ellen really wanted to do that kind of work. At least, Cliff was always complaining about it. Cliff would probably be very glad to have someone doing Ernie's job again.

So that was the plan, and the time to bring it up would be in the evening, after Father had eaten and rested for a while. The timing would have to be perfect and so would the things Cat would say. She would begin, she decided, by talking about Ernie.

The very next day, after waiting for just the right moment, she started in by saying, "I wonder how Ernie is." It was about an hour after dinner on Tuesday night and the whole family, except Ellen, was still sitting around the kitchen table. This winter, for some reason, the whole family had been staying in the warm kitchen after dinner instead of building a fire in the living-room fireplace the way they used to do.

Father had finished listening to the news on the radio, which had been mostly about the war in Spain and the floods in other parts of California. Both he and Cliff were reading the newspaper and Mama was mending. Ellen had gone to her room early, which was fine. Ellen wouldn't be any help, Cat felt sure. Even if she didn't like sweeping up and dusting at the store she'd be sure to find some reason to disagree with what Cat had to say. Like for instance the fact that Mr. Perkins was an Okie. Or what Ellen called an Okie, anyway, which seemed to be just about anyone who came from someplace else and didn't have much money.

No one looked up except Mama, so Cat had to say it again, louder, "I wonder how old Ernie is."

"Ernie's fine as far as I know," Father said. "I called the home just last month and they said Ernie was much the same."

"That's good," Cat said. "Ernie used to be a big help at the store, didn't he?"

131

"I'll say amen to that," Cliff said. "I didn't realize how much old Ernie did till I started having to do it myself. Sure wish we had him back."

Cat couldn't help smiling. Cliff had said just the right thing. "Well," she went on, "I don't see why you don't hire someone else to take Ernie's place. And I know just the person you ought to hire."

Father put down his newspaper and looked at Cat. "And who might that be?" he asked.

"It's this man named Perkins. He's been working on the Otis ranch until last week and the Perkins kids go to Brownwood School. You remember Zane Perkins? He's the one who's in my room, and he won the Winners' Grand Finale race and got all that Lions Club prize money for Brownwood. But Mr. Otis laid everybody off last week and so the Perkinses are going to have to move and they have this little girl who's kind of sick, and it sure would be swell if Mr. Perkins could get a job right here in Brownwood."

Father didn't say anything right away and after a minute Mama looked up from her mending. "This Perkins family, they're dust-bowl refugees?" she asked.

"Well—" Cat had begun when Cliff interrupted.

"Okies, she means. She wants to know if they're Okies. Are they Okies, Cat?"

"No, they aren't Okies," Cat said in a sassy tone of voice. "They're not even from Oklahoma, so how could they be Okies?"

"Oh, yeah? Where are they from, then?"

"Texas. They're from Texas."

Cliff laughed. "Big difference," he said.

"Catherine," Father said, "I hope you haven't said anything to these Perkins children about our hiring their father, because it just wouldn't be possible. For one thing, I doubt very much if Mr. Perkins would be a suitable employee for Kinsey's Hardware. And besides, if I were going to hire a stockman again, there's quite a few old Brownwood residents who would jump at the chance to get the job. And there's also the fact that a lot of my regular customers wouldn't understand my encouraging these transients to stay in the Brownwood area any longer than necessary. And, by the way . . ."

But Cat had stopped listening. Getting to her feet she shoved her chair back under the table very deliberately. Slowly and deliberately, in spite of the anger that was burning behind her eyes. She might have known. She might have known that Father wouldn't see it her way. Father never saw anything her way and probably never would. And she might also have known he would never spend a penny that he didn't have to, no matter what. And certainly not to please her. Certainly not a penny on anything that Catherine Kinsey wanted. "Never mind," she said between tight lips. "Just forget I mentioned it." Then she left the room.

In her own room Cat kicked off her shoes, put on her heavy winter robe, picked out a book, and lay down on her bed to read. It was about fifteen minutes later and she still hadn't been able to get her mind on what she was reading when someone knocked on the door. To her surprise it was Cliff.

"What do you want?" she said as rudely as she could,

feeling sure that he'd just thought of some clever way to tease her for having been stupid enough to think she could get a job for Mr. Perkins.

But he just stood there grinning for a minute before he pulled her desk chair over near the bed and sat down straddling its back.

"Look, kid," he said. "There's something I think you ought to know. So I thought I'd just fill you in a bit. Against orders, I might add, but so what? I don't think Kinsey senior is going to fire me at this point even if he should find out." He paused, shrugged, and grinned in a strange, almost embarrassed way. "But I must admit that I'd just as soon you didn't let him know I was the one who told you."

"Told me what?" Cat asked.

"That that grand old Brownwood institution, Kinsey's Hardware Emporium, has been teetering on the brink of bankruptcy for the last two or three years."

"Bankruptcy?"

"Going broke. Kinsey's Hardware has been just barely breaking even for a long time now. Sometimes not even that. And if the store goes under we'll lose it and probably the house too."

Cat was stunned. "I don't believe you," she said after a minute. "Father would have told me." Or would he? "Well, Mama would have, anyway."

"Lydia doesn't know either. Or at least she doesn't have any idea how bad things really are. Father won't tell her and he won't let me or Ellen tell her either. Seems to think she's not strong enough to bear the news. I tried to tell him she'd have a much better chance of developing some strength if he'd just start treating her like an adult. But you know Pa. There's no arguing with him. And he's dead set against anybody telling you. Says he wants you to have a carefree childhood."

"Carefree . . ." Cat said in a voice that she hardly recognized as her own. And then she didn't say anything else for a long time. Instead she just sat there staring. Cliff crossed his hands on the back of her chair, leaned his chin on them, and stared back. After a while, when he began to smile, she did, too, imitating that mocking, sarcastic Cliff Kinsey grin.

"And I've always thought he wouldn't spend any money on me because he just didn't like me very much," she said. She was trying to make it sound like a joke, but right in the middle of it there was a funny catch in her voice, almost like a sob.

"Yeah." Cliff had stopped grinning. "I had a notion that's what you thought. That's one of the reasons I decided to spill the beans. He cares about you a lot, kid, in his way. He just doesn't know how to show it. Never has known how. Not with Ellen and me when we were kids either. Used to try to do it with money when he had it, but now . . ." He shrugged again.

Cliff didn't say much more. After a while he got up off Cat's chair and left the room. At the door he turned around, rolled his eyes, and pretended to tip an imaginary hat. "Look," he said, "don't worry about it too much, kid. I've got a strong feeling this depression isn't going to last too much longer. At least that's what I think when I'm in a good mood."

It was a long time that night before Cat got to sleep. And

when she finally did she was awakened by a loud noise. At first, coming up out of a dream in which the whole Kinsey family was heading for Bakersfield in the old Model A, she didn't know what she'd heard. But then she recognized an all-too-familiar sound. It was raining again —hard, steady, driving rain.

TWENTY-FOUR

It was still raining when Cat went downstairs the next morning. In the kitchen Mama was listening to the radio as she made breakfast. As Cat finished setting the table she came close to telling Mama what Cliff had said the night before. Mama ought to know, just like she, Cat, ought to have known a long time ago. She'd be worried, of course, but there were worse things to worry about than bankruptcy.

That was one of the things Cat had decided when she was lying awake last night after Cliff's visit. For instance, thinking that Father wouldn't buy her a pony or a playhouse because he didn't like her as much as he did Ellen and Cliff was quite a lot worse. As a matter of fact, after thinking it over Cat had decided that she preferred bankruptcy to a lot of other problems. Because bankruptcy you could do something about.

The one thing that kept her from telling Mama right off was that she'd more or less promised Cliff she wouldn't let Father know who'd "spilled the beans." And if she told Mama—and Mama told Father—it was bound to come out that Cliff had been the one who'd told. So Cat decided to wait at least until she'd had a chance to talk to Cliff again before she said anything to anyone else. Besides, right at the moment Mama was very busy listening to the news about the flood.

The morning news on the radio was full of reports of flooding all up and down California and particularly in the southern part of the state. There wasn't any mention of problems in the foothills except that the news announcer did say that creeks and rivers all over the state were full to overflowing. Of course there was no mention of little old Coyote Creek, but Cat couldn't help thinking about it and wondering if, this time, it really was going to flood the grotto.

When Cliff came in he grinned at Cat and she grinned back and then shook her head when he made his eyebrows ask a question. A question that was clearly something like *You haven't been tattling, have you?*

A little later when everyone was around the table Cat found herself watching Father. He looked awfully tired. There were dark circles under his eyes, as if he hadn't been sleeping well. Worrying, probably, about the bankruptcy. And maybe worrying about whether Cat was having a carefree childhood? (That was really a new and fascinating idea.) She was still looking at Father, and imagining all the worries that were going on inside his head, when he looked up at her so suddenly that she surprised herself by smiling at him. Which seemed to surprise him too.

Breakfast was almost over when the phone rang. It was Mrs. Jayne calling to say that school had been canceled for the day. A tree had fallen during the night and knocked down some power lines and there were no lights or heat in the school building. The teachers were calling parents who had phones and Mr. Alessandro was at the school to send home any kids who didn't get the message. Like anyone whose family didn't have a phone, for instance. Cat wondered if the Perkins boys would walk all the way in from Okietown in the rain before they found out.

When breakfast was over and Father and Cliff and Ellen had gone to the store, Cat went to her room and looked out the window toward Brownwood Road. Sitting on the floor, as always, she watched the rain and the wet black ribbon of pavement that stretched away toward Okietown and the valley. If she saw the Perkinses going by she could run out and at least save them the rest of the trip into town. But nobody went by and after a while the rain died down to a drizzle and then stopped. It was then that she decided to make a trip to the grotto.

She didn't really think it would be flooded. The canyon floor was so wide in that area and the floor of the grotto was so much higher than the regular creek bed. But the fact remained that the grotto itself probably had been formed sometime in the far distant past by flood waters, and you couldn't be absolutely positive it wouldn't happen again. She would go to see, she decided, as soon as Mama started her afternoon nap.

In the coat closet by the back door she picked out a worn-out coat and a pair of rubber boots, both of which were actually Ellen's. The coat was an old one that Ellen only used to garden in, and the boots, which were quite a bit too big for Cat, had crackly places on both toes. But Cat's own boots, which she'd completely outgrown, had never been replaced. Cat nodded knowingly as she pulled them on, thinking about the new boots she'd probably have had long ago if it hadn't been for the bankruptcy problem. Cliff was certainly right. She really did need to know about family problems like that.

She started for the grotto that day soon after one o'clock. The pony pasture was a muddy marshland. The pasture where, it suddenly occurred to her, Father might someday, when the depression was over, let her keep a horse of her own. The steep path to the canyon floor was a slippery slide and the usually clear creek had become a noisy tumble of muddy water.

The trip down to the grotto was slow, complicated, and a little bit dangerous. There were places where Cat had to climb over boulders or forge a new trail along the side of the cliff face. And other places where the only route was through stretches of shallow water, wading along carefully in Ellen's leaky old boots. But the stairlike descent down the face of the cascade slope was unchanged—except wetter and a lot more slippery.

When Cat rounded the last boulder and the grotto thicket came into view, it was immediately apparent that the tunnel was underwater. Not a great deal of water, but enough so that crawling through it was going to be a soggy, muddy business.

She checked out the other entry then, the one she'd cleared when she brought in the playhouse panels, but the water was even deeper there and the vicious berry-vines had again twined up the face of the cliff. And of course she hadn't thought to bring her gloves or shears. So she returned to the tunnel, took off her boots, shoes, and socks, and put them on top of a fairly dry boulder. Then she tucked her coat up into the legs of her underpants, got down on her knees in the shallow, muddy water, and started to crawl. When she came out of the other end of the tunnel she was shocked to see that the grotto was flooded too.

The water wasn't deep on the grotto floor, but at least an inch or two of muddy water was everywhere. All of Cat's treasures on the high shelves at the back of the grotto were safe, high above water level, but little waves of muddy water were lapping at the cottage door. Splashing barefoot through the cold, slimy mud Cat hurried to the door and jerked it open. Lillybelle's bed was underwater.

As she waded across the cottage floor, waves created by her splashing feet lapped up over the legs and slats of the doll crib. It wasn't until she was bending over it that she realized it was empty. There were no blankets or mattress in the bed and no Lillybelle.

No Lillybelle. The startling fact had just begun to sink in when suddenly Cat saw her. Not in her crib but still there in the cottage. Still wrapped, not only in her pink blanket, but also in Sammy's blue dress, she was lying safely on the stone ledge high above water level. Someone had been to the cottage since Cat was last there and had moved Lillybelle up to a safer, drier place. Cat didn't try to guess who it was that had been there. For some reason she didn't want to know. Didn't want to know who had come through the rain and flood, all the way to the grotto, just to put someone else's doll up out of harm's way.

She stood perfectly still for a while staring at Lillybelle before she took her off the ledge and buttoned her, still wrapped in the dress and blanket, inside her coat. It was a tight fit but not too tight. Since it was actually a grown-up woman's coat there was enough room in the chest to hold a good-sized doll.

141

Then Cat crawled back out through the flooded tunnel, shoved her muddy feet back into her socks, shoes, and boots—and headed downstream. She certainly hadn't planned to visit Okietown when she left home, or even when she was in the cottage. In fact, it wasn't until she was under way, climbing over boulders and splashing through shallow overflows, that she asked herself why on earth she was doing it. For one thing it was getting late. It had taken much longer to reach the grotto than usual. The heavy, sunless sky was already darkening and the shadows were becoming long and dark. "I just have to say good-bye," she told herself. "I have to tell them all good-bye. I just *have* to."

But there was another reason. Looking down to where Lillybelle's stiff, starchy ringlets could be seen peeking out from inside the tightly buttoned coat, Cat suddenly knew the real reason she was going. To give Lillybelle to Sammy to take with her to Bakersfield or wherever the Perkinses might go next.

Okietown was an almost deserted sea of mud. The outhouse was still there, tipped slightly to one side now, and the ugly piles of trash were even larger. But most of the tents were gone, and the shanties, too, except for, here and there, a rusty tin wall or a soggy heap of cardboard. But the Perkinses' tent was still where it had been. And smoke was coming from the chimney in one of the old workers' cabins.

Cat was making her way through the deep mud of the camp road when she became aware of clanking noises and the sound of voices coming from what had been the Perkins family's tent. She approached cautiously. In the light of a lamp that hung from the roof beam she could see that the tent was empty now except for two men and a car. The Studebaker had been turned so that its open hood was inside the tent. Beside it, on the ground, was what seemed to be most of its motor. The two men, dressed in wet and greasy overalls, were crouching over the pile of engine parts.

"Er, hello," Cat said. "Could I—could you tell me . . ." One of the men, tall, with a thin face and gray-blond hair, got to his feet and stared in her direction.

"Yeah?" he asked. Only one word but something, the tone of his voice or the expression in his eyes, said other, more desperate things.

"The P-P-Perkinses," Cat stammered. "Are they still here?"

The man's strange, tormented stare didn't change. "Who are you?" he asked.

"I'm Catherine Kinsey," Cat said. "I came to see Sammy. Sammy Perkins."

The man shook his head, still staring at Cat in the strange unseeing way. Then he pointed, flinging out an arm toward the closest of the old workers' cabins, and went back to whatever he'd been doing to the pile of engine parts.

The one-room cabin was made of weathered, unpainted wood, and stood up on a foundation of stiltlike legs. Three rickety wooden steps led to the only door. A murmur of voices came from inside the cabin. When Cat knocked the voices stopped and a moment later Roddy Perkins opened the door. Roddy's nose was running. His eyes were red and swollen and his face was wet with tears.

The room was very hot and smelled of woodsmoke, kerosene, and unwashed clothing. Mrs. Perkins was there and

Spence and Zane. Zane was on his knees by the potbellied wood stove, pushing a small log in among the flames. Spence, who was standing near an oilcloth-covered table on which a kerosene lamp was burning, had been crying too. Mrs. Perkins was kneeling beside a mattress on the floor.

Roddy grabbed Cat's arm, pulled her into the room, and closed the door behind her. Mrs. Perkins glanced up briefly but then turned away as if Cat's presence had failed to register. As if her blank, unfocused eyes were full of something so terrible, they had become blind to anything else.

Sammy was lying on the mattress, her head and shoulders propped up on a pile of blankets. Her eyes were closed. Her cheeks were flushed and she was breathing in noisy little gasps. Cat was still staring, when Zane grabbed her arm and pulled her back toward the door.

"Sammy . . . ?" Cat started to ask, but Zane was already answering her question.

"She's took real bad," Zane said. "Ma thinks it's pneumonia."

TWENTY-FIVE

"Pneumonia." Cat stared at Sammy. She was horror-stricken, unbelieving. "But—but I thought she was getting better. Nobody told me."

"Yeah, she was. But she snuck out and went up the creek. Me and Spence and Roddy was at school and Ma and Pa didn't know about—you know—about your cave place and that doll she sets such store by. So they didn't know where to look for her. She was gone a long time. I found her when I got back after school. On her way home, all wet and turrible cold. She started getting worse that night, but she wasn't took real bad till yesterday."

Cat felt a sudden pain, as if something sharp had stabbed deep into her chest. She knew where Sammy had been and why. And she knew now, for certain, who had put Lillybelle up on the ledge. The pain was so bad, she clutched her chest, wrapping her arms tightly around herself—*and* the sharp bulge that was Lillybelle. Frantically unbuttoning her coat she held the doll out to Zane.

"Here," she said, her voice out of control, high and wailing, "take it. I brought it for her. I brought it for Sammy. For her to keep."

It wasn't until that moment that she remembered about

Zane and the chewing gum. And how Zane felt about the Perkinses not being beggars. She didn't care, though. She didn't care what Zane Perkins thought. She was going to give Lillybelle to Sammy no matter what Zane—

But Zane didn't argue or even hesitate. Instead he took the doll out of Cat's hands and went over to kneel beside Sammy's bed. At first, when he whispered in her ear, her eyelids only fluttered, but after he whispered again they opened. When Zane held the doll up in front of her face, her lips curved in just a flicker of a smile before they parted in another quick gasping breath. Zane was still whispering as he tucked Lillybelle under the blanket, and again a smile trembled on Sammy's lips and then died away.

The pain in Cat's chest had spread to her throat and her eyes were wet and hot. Angrily, she brushed her hand across her face. She wasn't going to cry. Crying was useless. There had to be something better to do than stand around and cry. There had to be. . . .

"Mrs. Perkins," she said, "why don't you take her to the doctor? I'll bet Dr. Wilson could help her. Dr. Wilson's real good with pneumonia. I'll bet if you took Sammy to . . ."

Mrs. Perkins was nodding her head. "We're going to," she said. "Jist as soon as Pa and Elmer gets the car runnin' we're goin' to take her in to Brownwood."

"But"—Cat stared at Mrs. Perkins in dismay—"but the car's still all torn up. There's a big chunk of it still sitting on the ground. How soon is it going to be running?"

Mrs. Perkins shook her head. "I dunno." She threw her arms out wildly in a despairing gesture. "Yesterday Elmer was sayin' it would be runnin' for sure by this mornin'. Him and Pa worked most all night on it. But now some-

146

thin' else has went wrong." Mrs. Perkins's rough, work-worn hands were moving continually as she spoke, twisting and grasping each other over and over again. "And everybody's moved on now 'cept us and Elmer. Nobody's here with a car to take Sammy into town, or even to go lookin' for help."

"I was goin' to go," Zane said. "I was goin' to go to Brownwood to look for a doctor. But Pa wouldn't let me." Cat could hear the familiar fierceness in his voice as he went on. "Pa said it warn't no use. Said no doctor was goin' to drive way out here on the say-so of some Okie kid."

Cat stared at him. "I'll go," she said. "If I tell Dr. Wilson how sick Sammy is, I'll bet he'll come."

For a moment something like hope shone in Mrs. Perkins's eyes. But then she shook her head. "It's a long way into Brownwood. Nigh on five mile, ain't it? It'll take you a long time to go that fer."

Cat shook her head. "I can run fast. And it's not quite that far to my house. I can phone from there. I can call from my house and if Dr. Wilson's in his office I just know he'll drive out here in his car."

Mrs. Perkins nodded and then shook her head. "I don't know," she said. "I jist don't know. Like as not the doctor won't come. And it's goin' to be dark 'fore long and it's such a fer piece and . . ."

"I'll go with her," Zane said. "All right, Ma? Is it all right if I go too?"

But Mrs. Perkins wasn't listening. Sammy's breathing had quickened and every gasp seemed to be a desperate struggle against suffocation. Her mother knelt beside the bed as the frantic rasping gasp went on and on. With the sound of Sammy's tortured breathing filling her ears, Cat ran for the door. She was on her way down the rickety wooden steps when the cabin door slammed again and Zane was right behind her.

"Which way you goin' to go?" he said when he caught up.

Cat stopped. "What do you mean, which way?"

"I mean, up the canyon, or along the road? Up the canyon is shortest, ain't it?"

"Shortest, maybe, but not the fastest. Not with all the flooding, anyway. I came down the canyon and it took a long time. The road will be a lot faster."

Zane nodded sharply. "Awright," he said, "let's go."

It was slow going in the deep mud of the unpaved trail that led from Okietown to the Brownwood road. Slow, sloppy going with thick mud splashing up at every step of Zane's bare feet, and with Cat struggling to keep her footing in her floppy, too-big boots. When they reached the road she sat down and began to tug on one of the boots.

"Whatcha doin' now? You gonna carry them things?" Zane had stopped, too, and was watching while she tried to get a grip on the mud-coated boot.

"No," Cat said. "I'm going to throw them away. Or hide them somewhere. I can't run in these things."

"Guess not," Zane said. Grabbing her foot he quickly jerked off one boot, and then the other. Both her shoes came off, too, and she quickly put them back on while Zane stashed the boots under a bush beside the road. Then they began to run in earnest.

Overhead the clouds still hung low. The air was stony cold and to the east the sky was darkening toward twilight. But even in the cold Cat could feel the sweat beginning to trickle down her cheeks and the backs of her legs. Underfoot, however, the surface of the old blacktop road was almost dry and fairly smooth except for an occasional pothole. A smooth, even racetrack stretching out endlessly in front of them.

But it wasn't a race at first. At first they ran side by side, fast but not pushing it. Beside her Zane's strides covered more ground than Cat's did, but hers were smoother and more efficient. They had passed the rise beyond the bridge and were still running side by side when they looked at each other. Just one long, hard, testing look, and the race began.

Zane's strides lengthened, his long legs angling up and down, up and down, like the parts of some awkward but fast-moving machine. Cat ran faster, too, feeling the familiar drive to win, and the deeper and more mysterious urge to run and keep running. Feeling the sure, swift flow of muscle, the strong, even beat of her heart, and the aching need to run fast and free. She was moving smoothly and easily—and faster perhaps than she had ever run before.

But Zane was faster. Not a lot faster, but enough so that he gradually pulled out and away. As they passed the dead orchard he was a few feet ahead, and by the time they reached the ruins of the old Ferris house he was out in front by several yards.

Cat kept running, pushing her aching legs and trying to ignore the fire that had begun to burn in her lungs. Her mind, as always soothed and quieted by the running, was not yet quieted enough. The need to win was gone, but the pain in her lungs had not yet drowned the pain for

Sammy. For Sammy dying of pneumonia because she, Cat Kinsey, had been too late. Had given her Lillybelle too late. She couldn't run fast enough to forget about that.

They were almost to the last turn in the road before the high valley when she began to catch up. Zane was slowing down. His stride had become uneven, his legs wavering and wobbly. Cat drew closer and closer. The gap between them had narrowed to a few steps when Zane faltered, staggered—and fell to his knees.

Zane's face was wet with sweat and dead white, except for a greenish tinge around his eyes and mouth. As Cat stopped beside him he began to vomit. He retched painfully over and over again but only a thin stream of whitish fluid came from his mouth. When the retching finally ended he wiped his mouth with the sleeve of his shirt and looked up at Cat. "Go on," he gasped. "Go on and get the doctor. I cain't go no farther."

"But—but . . ." Cat stammered.

"Go on, I'm tellin' you—get out of here—I'll be awright in a minute."

Cat started to back away and then came back. "My house is just up around the next turn," she said.

"Yeah." Zane nodded, still gasping. "I know—where— you live."

"I'm going there to phone," Cat said. "You come there, too, soon as you can. Okay?"

"Okay," Zane gasped.

Cat went on running.

TWENTY-SIX

The moment Cat turned off old Brownwood Road into the Kinseys' long, curving driveway she heard someone calling. And then she saw her. Mama was standing on the front porch peering out into the semidarkness and calling in her faint, childish voice, "Cathy—Catherine—Cathy." Over and over and over again in a weak, tired way, as if she'd been standing there calling for a long time.

Cat tried to answer but only a painful rasping sound came up from her aching lungs. So she just went on running until she staggered, gasping and panting, into the rectangle of light that spilled out from the open door.

Mama ran to meet her. "Cathy, oh, thank God. Where have you been? Oh, my God, Cathy. What happened to you?"

As Cat struggled up the stairs Mama was clinging to her, holding her back. "What happened? Where have you been?" she kept repeating. Cat shoved the clinging arms away impatiently, trying to get past her and down the hall to the telephone.

It wasn't until she caught a glimpse of herself in the oval mirror of the hall tree that she began to understand why

Mama seemed so horrified. For a moment the reflection in the mirror hardly looked like Cat Kinsey.

What Cat saw was a strange, outlandish creature whose red-blotched face dripped with sweat and whose mouth hung open. A creature who panted in noisy gasps like some exhausted animal, and whose face, hands, and legs were spotted, smeared, and coated with mud. "I'm all right," she managed to gasp. "Just tired. Been running—long way."

"But where were you?" Mama was following close behind her as she staggered down the hall and collapsed onto the bench by the phone table. "Where did you go? When I woke up you were gone and I kept thinking you'd be back, but you didn't come, and I was so worried. You mustn't do things like this to me, Cathy. You know I'm not well and—"

"Tell you—later. Got to phone now. Phone Dr. Wilson."

"Phone Dr. Wilson? Cathy, are you sick? Are you hurt? Cathy, what happened . . . ?"

Shutting out the sound of Mama's wailing voice Cat dialed and, as she waited for an answer, prayed, "Be there, Dr. Wilson. Dear God, please let him be there."

The phone rang and rang and at last there was a click at the other end of the line and Dr. Wilson's warm, familiar voice said, "Brownwood Clinic. Dr. Wilson speaking."

"It's Catherine Kinsey." Fighting her still air-starved lungs and racing heart Cat began to babble. "You've got to come, Dr. Wilson. I mean you've got to go out to Okietown. Sammy's terribly sick. Samantha Perkins. She's a little girl. Only five years old. She's about to die, Dr. Wilson. She can't breathe. And there's no car—and everybody's gone—except the Perkinses and their car's broken and . . ." She paused. "Dr. Wilson. Can you come? Right away?"

"Cathy?" As always Dr. Wilson's voice was calm and slow. Maddeningly slow. "What is it, child? I can't understand you."

She started again. Repeating all of it, about Sammy and how sick she was. She was about to begin all over again for the third time when she suddenly realized that something had changed. Mama, who had continued to wail softly in the background, had suddenly become very quiet. Behind Cat's back there was a listening kind of silence. When she turned around Father was standing beside Mama, and Cliff and Ellen were behind him.

"Father," she stammered, "I was calling Dr. Wilson. I was telling him—"

Father nodded. "I heard what you were telling him, Catherine." He stepped forward, holding out his hand for the receiver. "I don't think—"

At that moment the front door flew open with a bang and Zane Perkins staggered into the hall. A wild-eyed, barefoot, mud-smeared Zane who burst through the door, waving his arms and gasping. He lunged forward to the foot of the stairs and, clutching the newel post to keep from falling, hung there while strange noises came from his open mouth.

Father stared at Zane and then, grabbing Cat's arm, he took the phone away from her. Cat reached for it despairingly but Father only turned away. "Hello, John," he said, "Charles Kinsey here." There was a pause, then, "Yes, I heard part of it. No. I don't know what it's all about. At

153

least no more than you do. I just got home a few minutes ago." Another pause. "No. No, I don't think so. I don't see why you should—"

Cat grabbed Father's arm and stared up into his face. For a long moment he looked down at her and then over to where Zane was still clutching the newel post and making strange moaning noises as he tried to say something.

"Father"—Ellen's high-pitched voice drowned out the sound of Zane's efforts to speak—"I don't see why we or the doctor should get ourselves involved in these people's lives. After all, it was their choice to . . ."

Father looked at Ellen and then back at Cat. Then he turned his back on Ellen and said to Dr. Wilson, "Well, I hate to ask you to but it does seem we have some kind of an emergency here." He looked at his watch. "Right at your suppertime, too, I imagine. But it might be . . ."

There was another long pause while the faint buzz of Dr. Wilson's voice could be heard talking slowly and calmly at the other end of the line. At last Father went on, "Well, it's up to you, John. Yes. Stop by our place first. Perhaps I'll know more by then. See you shortly, then."

Dr. Wilson was coming. Cat felt a great lightening as if a terrible dark cloud through which she had been struggling, a cloud so thick and airless that she could hardly breathe, had suddenly floated up and away. She was turning toward Zane to see if he had heard and understood that Dr. Wilson was coming, when everything began to whirl. The hall tree and the mirror and the faces of Mama, Father, Cliff, Ellen, and Zane seemed to be drifting slowly around her in circles, and then everything went dark.

The next thing she knew she was in Father's arms. Father was carrying her up the stairs while Mama ran beside them crying and calling her name over and over again.

Cat began to struggle. "Put me down," she said. "I want to get down. I have to . . ." But the dim swirling sensation returned then and, frightened, she lay still. Father went on climbing the stairs and then down the hall to her room. As he was putting her down on her bed she tried again. Pushing herself to a sitting position she said, "Zane?"

"Cliff is looking after the boy," Father said.

Cat nodded and allowed herself to be pushed back down. Cliff would take good care of Zane.

"Father," she said, "we ran all the way from Okietown, Zane and I. All the way."

"Yes," he said, "I know." For a moment he stood over the bed, looking down at her. As always his face was quiet, his mouth still and controlled and his eyes shadowed. But somehow the shadows weren't as dense, and Cat sensed something different behind them. Something she'd never seen before—or ever looked for. "That's a very long way to run," he said. "You're a strong young lady, Catherine. A good, strong young lady."

Father went out then and Mama helped Cat get cleaned up and into bed. All that time, while Mama was bathing her and getting her into her nightgown, Cat's mind seemed to be stuck like a phonograph needle on a ruined record, repeating and repeating the same thing—running, running, running. All that would stay in her head was the running. In her head and in her legs and arms too. Her muscles could still feel it, and when she closed her eyes the running went on behind her eyelids. And the same words kept whispering through her mind. "We ran all the way from Okietown. All the way."

After a long time the voice in her mind whispered, "Zane ran faster," but that didn't seem to matter all that much. What mattered was—for a moment she could hardly remember, but then it came back. Sammy and pneumonia and—*Dr. Wilson was coming.* Cat sighed deeply and went to sleep.

TWENTY-SEVEN

Cat woke with a start the next morning as if to the sound of a whispering voice. But the voice had been inside her head. The whisper said, *Go back to sleep. Something terrible happened. Go back where it can't reach you.* But she ignored the warning and opened her eyes. A moment later, still in her nightgown, she was running down the stairs thinking *How could I have slept? How could I?*

Mama was making coffee as Cat burst through the kitchen door. "Sammy," she shouted. "Where's Sammy? How is she? I have to call Dr. Wilson."

Mama put down the coffeepot and pushed Cat into a chair. "Cathy, sit down," she said. "You shouldn't be out of bed. You fainted last night. You're not well."

"I'm fine," Cat said, struggling to stand up. She'd almost forgotten about the fainting—but it didn't matter. "I'm fine now," she said. "I have to call—"

"Cathy, listen to me. Father called Dr. Wilson a few minutes ago. She's all right. The little girl is all right."

"Sammy's all right?" Relief, so sharp and sudden it was almost painful, flooded over her. She closed her eyes and let her head fall back against the chair.

"Well, not entirely perhaps," Mama said. "The doctor said she is still very ill but she's holding her own."

Cat's eyes flew open. "Holding her own? What does that mean?"

"It means she's a fighter," Father said. He and Cliff had come into the kitchen while Cat's eyes were closed. "According to Dr. Wilson she's a real fighter. She's at the clinic and the doctor and Mrs. Wilson have been up with her most of the night. Doc says it was nip and tuck for a while but she's doing better this morning. Responding to treatment." Father came over and put his hand on Cat's shoulder. "He also said that she undoubtedly would have died if he hadn't reached her when he did. He says you saved her life, Catherine."

Cat nodded. "And Zane too. How is Zane? He was sick too."

"I think he's fine," Cliff said. "I think it was only exhaustion. And hunger, perhaps. I got him to eat a little last night. By the time Dr. Wilson arrived he seemed to be pretty much back to normal. He rode out to the camp with the doc to show him the way."

"And where are they now—the rest of the Perkinses?"

"Well, I suppose the mother—Mrs. Perkins, is it?—is at the clinic," Father said. "Dr. Wilson said she rode in with him and the child last night. But I gather the rest of the family are still out at the camp."

Still at the camp. Still out there in that terrible, lonely, deserted mudhole. With no way to leave and maybe not even any food. Cat was sitting silently, her mind swamped with dark images, when she realized a new voice was talking to her. Talking and asking questions. It was Ellen.

158

Ellen was full of questions that morning. She wanted to know how Cat happened to know the Perkins family and how on earth she happened to be at the Okie camp last night. And what was she thinking of to go to a place like that all by herself and after dark at that? What on earth was she thinking of?

"It wasn't after dark when I went there," Cat said. "It just got that way later." Then she went on and tried to explain *why* she went there by telling how she and Sammy had met because they both played in the canyon. And how they had become friends and how when she, Cat, had heard that the Perkinses were leaving she decided to go to the camp to tell them good-bye.

She made it into a very short story, leaving out most of the important details, and ignoring Ellen's disapproving gasps. But even so the telling seemed to take a lot of energy. By the time she finished she felt exhausted and it must have shown, because Mama began to fuss about how tired she looked and how she should go right back to bed.

"I'll bring your breakfast up later," Mama said.

Cat tried to say she was perfectly all right but Father sided with Mama. "All right," Cat said, "I'll go back to bed. But someone has to go out to the camp and tell them. Someone just *has* to go out there this minute and tell the rest of the family that Sammy is still alive."

They just stood there staring at her, all four of them, and suddenly she was angry. She wanted to scream at them and run out of the room but instead she took a deep breath and said calmly, "Well, if nobody else is going to do it I'm going to go right out that door this minute and go do it myself."

Cliff began to laugh and that really made her angry—

just for a moment. But then she looked down at herself, standing there with her hands on her hips, barefoot and still in her nightgown. She could see what Cliff was laughing about and for the tiniest moment she grinned back. But that didn't change what had to be done. "Here I go," she said, and headed for the door, but Father grabbed her arm. He was smiling too.

"You're quite right, Catherine," he said. "They must be told, of course. Cliff will drive out there immediately and let them know." He turned to Cliff. "You can be back before eight if you hurry."

"Of course, Cliff will do it," Cliff said. "Cliff will drive out to Okietown immediately. Before breakfast." He sounded sarcastic, but he grinned at Cat as he grabbed a piece of toast from the table on his way out the door.

Back in her room Cat watched from the window as the old Model A sputtered down the driveway and headed north. She got back into bed and thought about the Model A—and how much she'd always hated it. And hated Father for not buying them a decent car. And of course that led to thinking about the bankruptcy.

She was surprised to realize that she hadn't worried about it much, but of course there hadn't been a whole lot of time. So many things had happened since Tuesday when Cliff told her. She'd probably worry about it more later. There would be a lot to think about later, but in the meantime there were more important things to consider.

It wasn't raining but it was another cold, gray day. Cat got out of bed again and looked up at the dark, dreary clouds. In her mind's eye she could see the piles of trash and the pitiful wooden shacks, and most of all she could see Zane and Spence and the others not knowing. Still not even knowing whether Sammy was alive.

Cliff didn't come back in a half hour, or in an hour. After a while Mama came up with Cat's breakfast and said that Father and Ellen had decided to walk into town to open the store. It was a good thing they did, because it was almost noon before the Model A chugged down the drive. When Cat heard the familiar sound she jumped out of bed and ran downstairs so quickly she met Cliff as he came in the back door. His shoes and pants were muddy and he was worried about being so late, but he seemed to be in a good mood. Cat grabbed his arm and hung on.

"All right. All right," he said. "I'll tell you all about it. It was a good thing I went. They hadn't heard about Sammy. Didn't know whether she was dead or alive." He stopped, shaking his head as if in disbelief. "The boys ran out to meet me, but then it was like they didn't want to hear what I had to say. Afraid it might be bad news, I guess. But they were awfully glad when it wasn't."

Cliff glanced at his watch. "I stayed a lot longer than I should have. Turned out they needed another spark plug for the Studebaker. So I drove Mr. Perkins into town and helped him get one. And then I drove him back out there and helped out a bit until they got the old crate running."

Cliff looked down then at Cat's hands still clutching his arm and said, "Unhand me, kid. I've got to get cleaned up and down to the store before the old man has a conniption fit."

The next day Cat went back to school. The Perkinses weren't there and no one seemed to know anything about them. So that night after dinner she called the Wilson residence. Not the clinic, but the house on Pine Street where the Wilsons lived. The doctor's wife answered the phone. Mrs. Wilson was full of information.

Sammy was still making good progress. The rest of the Perkins family had kind of camped in the Wilsons' garage last night but in a day or two they were going to leave for Bakersfield. All of them except Sammy, of course, and Mrs. Perkins. Sammy and Mrs. Perkins would stay there in the clinic until Sammy was strong enough to travel and then they would go on to Bakersfield, too, by bus.

"That's awful," Cat said.

"What's awful, dear?" Mrs. Wilson said.

"That they're going off to Bakersfield without even knowing if they can get work there, or find a place to live or . . ."

"I know, dear," Mrs. Wilson said. "But I think things might work out for them there. John talked to Reverend Booker yesterday about the Perkinses, and the reverend called his brother. It just so happens that Reverend Booker has a brother who works for the government in that area. His agency has been building places for dust-bowl immigrants to live. Just camps, really, but the tents have wooden floors and there are washrooms and showers. Reverend Booker's brother says they can move right into one of the camps. And once they get there he's going to see what he can do to help Mr. Perkins find work."

Cat thanked Mrs. Wilson and hung up. She supposed Reverend Booker's brother and the government camp made things a little bit better—but not much. She still

162

thought it was a dumb thing for the Perkinses to do. *Dumb* to go off all that way without knowing what they were getting into. She surely did wish she could see Zane Perkins just for a minute so she could tell him so.

TWENTY-EIGHT

The next day was Saturday and it got off to a very bad start. During breakfast Father and Cliff got into one of their church arguments. This time it started because Cliff mentioned that Reverend Booker was going to take up a collection in church to help with the Perkinses' bill at the clinic.

Cliff should have known better. Mentioning the Reverend Booker to Father, particularly before he'd had his first cup of coffee in the morning, was just like waving a red flag at a bull. Ellen joined in on Father's side, of course, Mama's eyes were beginning to get red, and Cat was gulping down her oatmeal so she could get out of there, when suddenly there was a knock on the back door. Father and Cliff, who were both talking at once, stopped in mid-sentence.

"Who could that be this hour of the morning?" Ellen said.

But then Cliff remembered that his friend Bud Jackson had promised to stop by to return an inner-tube mending kit he'd borrowed. Cliff was getting out of his chair when Father said, "Sit down, Clifford. Catherine can go. I want to finish the point I was making. Go to the door, Catherine."

So it was Cat who went to the door, but the person who had knocked wasn't Bud Jackson after all. It was Zane Perkins. Zane Perkins, barefoot and tattered as usual, but a good deal cleaner than he'd been the last time Cat had seen him.

"Howdy, Cat Kinsey," he said, grinning. His grin was the usual too. Wide and ornery.

Cat closed the door behind her, quickly and tightly. "I— I thought you were on your way to Bakersfield."

He nodded. "Leavin' right soon," he said. "This afternoon, like as not, if nothin' else breaks down."

Then he went on grinning and staring until Cat began to get mad. Sticking out her chin she said, "What are you staring at?"

"Not a thing," he said. "Not a gol-durned thing. Oh, I almost fergot. I brung you something." Reaching in his overall bib pocket he brought out a small linen handkerchief. "Here"—he held it out to her—"it's for you. From my ma. She worked it for you."

When Cat unfolded the handkerchief she saw that the letters *C.K.* had been embroidered in one corner. "Ma worked it while she was sittin' up nights with Sammy," Zane said. "She ast me to bring it over to you 'fore we left today."

"Thank you," Cat said. "I mean, would you tell your ma thank you for me?"

"I'll tell her," Zane said. "Oh, yeah. Got somethin' else for you too." He pulled a wrinkled scrap of paper out of another pocket. "This here's from Sammy. It's a letter."

"Can Sammy write?"

"Naw. Not really. But she told me what to say. I writ it down for her."

In large, messy handwriting the letter said:

Dear Cat,
Please come see me at the clinic. Lilly Bell says howdy.
                                        Love,
                                        Sammy Perkins

"Doc Wilson says she can have visitors now," Zane said. "She and Ma are going to be here for a while. Maybe a week or so. Room three at the clinic."

Cat said she would visit Sammy real soon. After that nobody said anything for quite a while. Zane looked off toward the road and then up at the sky and Cat studied the note and the handkerchief. But then, just as Zane started to say something, Cat suddenly remembered what she'd wanted to tell him if she saw him again. They both started talking at once but it was Cat who kept going.

"Hey," she said, "I just wanted to tell you that I think it's real dumb going off to Bakersfield the way you are. I don't think you should go. I mean, down there where you don't know anybody and there probably isn't any work— and the schools are a lot worse than Brownwood."

Zane chuckled in that maddening way he had. "How do you know the schools are worse?"

Cat smiled triumphantly. "Because Spence told me so. He told me how bad they were at the other place where you were."

He nodded. "Yeah, that school in Cottonville was purty bad, all right. But maybe we're going to go to a real good

166

school the Reverend Booker's brother knows about. Specially for camp kids."

"Maybe?" Cat said scornfully. "Just maybe?"

"Yeah, maybe. Maybe's better'n nothin'."

The conversation bogged down again then for a while until, all of a sudden, Zane said, "Oh, yeah. I wanted to tell you. You know what I said about the depression and your Pa's store and all?"

Cat nodded, a small, grudging nod.

"Well, I had no call to say somethin' like that. Your Pa's store's doin' fine, like as not."

"No, it's not!" Cat said angrily. "It's practically bankrupt."

"Is that right?" Zane looked solemn. Not teasing or obnoxious for once, but just solemn and interested. "Well, that's a real pity," he said. "But look-a-here. You shouldn't ought to worry 'bout it, 'cause things are goin' to get better soon. My pa was talkin' to Doc Wilson yesterday and Doc Wilson said he thinks this here depression's almost over. And right soon now things is going to start gettin' better for everybody. And Pa says that must be true, 'cause Doc Wilson knows more than jist 'bout anybody."

"Umm," Cat said. "Cliff says so too. At least that's what he says when he's in a good mood."

They looked at each other then, and right at the very same instant—they smiled. Zane took a step closer. "Look," he said, "I'm going to come back to Brownwood someday, sure as shootin'. I'm comin' back because I like . . ." He looked at Cat sideways and then up at the sky and then at Cat again. Then he kind of sighed and shrugged and said, "I like this here town." Then he said, "Well, then—so long, and—I'll be seein' you."

167

He whirled around and started off down the driveway and then, without even pausing, he whirled around again and came right back. "About that there race we had," he said, "you won. You were the one who got to the finish line."

Cat shook her head. Her throat suddenly felt so stiff she could only say, "No. You're faster."

He chuckled. "For the short haul, maybe. Anyways"— he paused and then reached out suddenly and shook Cat's hand—"anyways, you keep on runnin', Cat Kinsey." Then he started off down the driveway, and this time he kept going.

When Cat opened the kitchen door the argument about churches hadn't ended, and it didn't sound like it was about to anytime soon. Everyone was still talking at once, except for Mama, who had started to cry. Nobody noticed Cat, so she backed out of the room, closed the door behind her, and ran around the house. She went in the front door and up the stairs to her room at full speed. So fast that she reached her window in time to catch a last glimpse of Zane as he turned toward town on the Old Brownwood Road.

"You, too, Zane Perkins," she whispered. "You keep on running too."